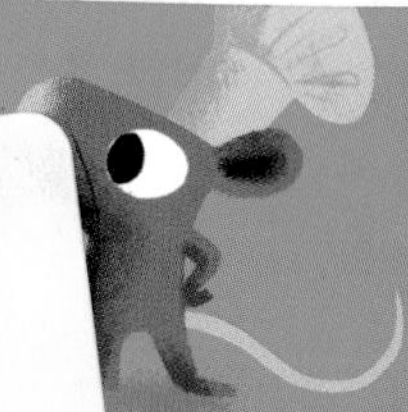

Also look for:

BOBO AND PUP-PUP: WE LOVE BUBBLES!

BOBO and PUP-PUP

LET'S MAKE CAKE!

by Vikram Madan
illustrated by Nicola Slater

A STEPPING STONE BOOK™

Random House 🏠 New York

For Jahnvi and Jawahar, who make me proud every day
—V.M.

To Leo and Finn
—N.S.

Text copyright © 2021 by Vikram Madan
Cover art and interior illustrations copyright © 2021 by Nicola Slater

All rights reserved. Published in the United States by Random House Children's Books,
a division of Penguin Random House LLC, New York.

Random House and the colophon are registered trademarks and A Stepping Stone Book
and the colophon are trademarks of Penguin Random House LLC.

Visit us on the Web!
rhcbooks.com

Educators and librarians, for a variety of teaching tools, visit us at RHTeachersLibrarians.com

Library of Congress Cataloging-in-Publication Data is available upon request.
ISBN 978-0-593-12068-2 (hardcover) | ISBN 978-0-593-12069-9 (library binding) |
ISBN 978-0-593-12070-5 (ebook)

PRINTED IN THE UNITED STATES OF AMERICA
10 9 8 7 6 5 4 3
First Edition

Contents

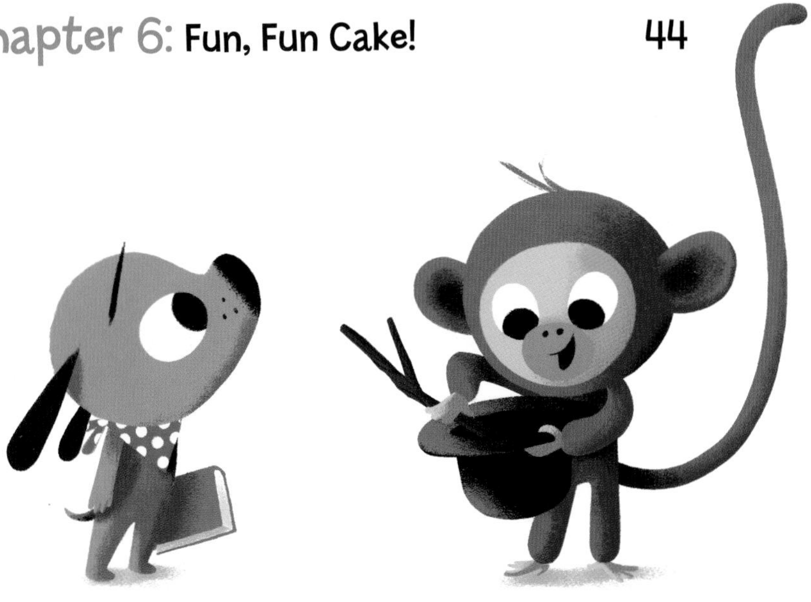

Chapter 1
Cake, Cake, Cake!

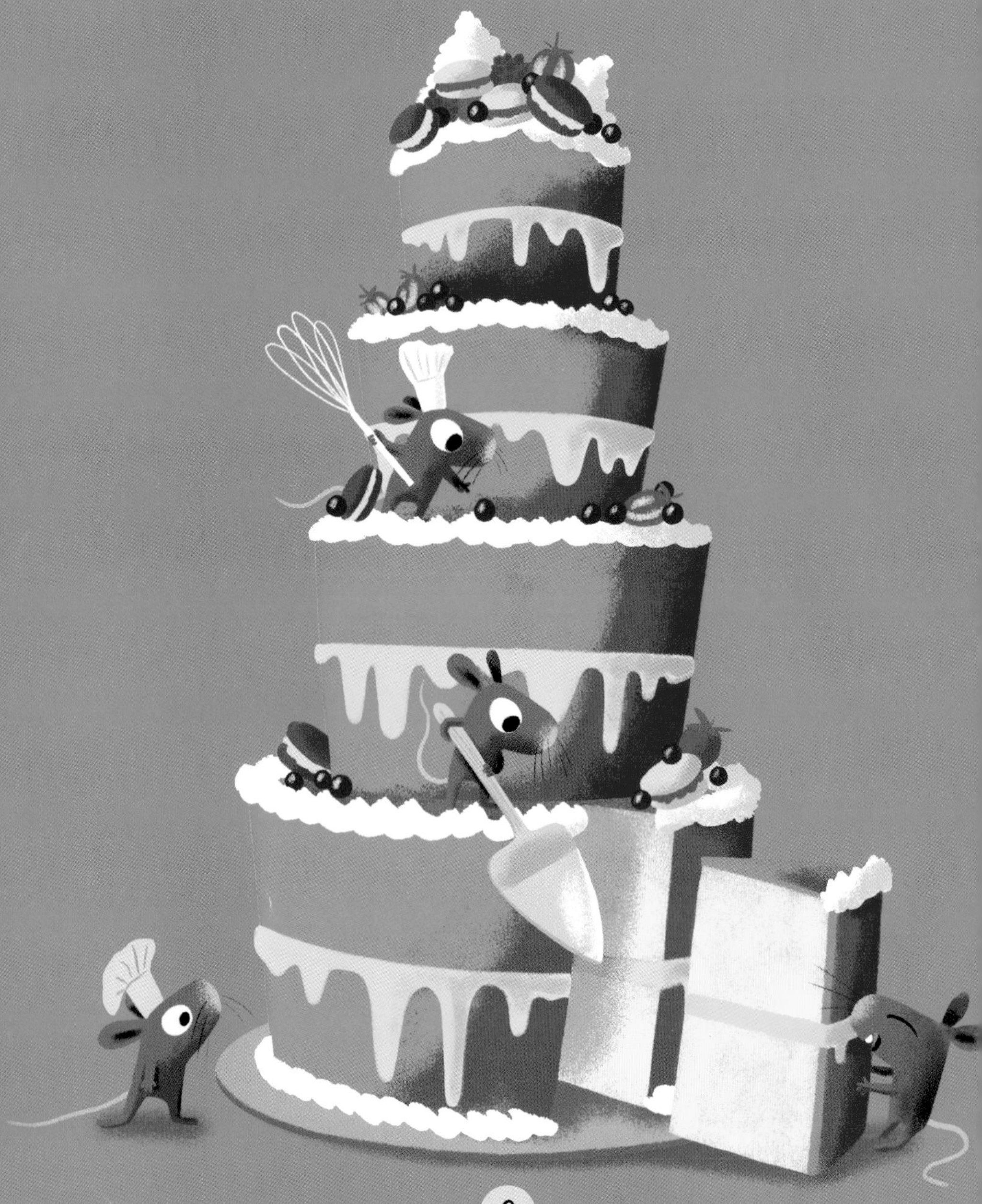

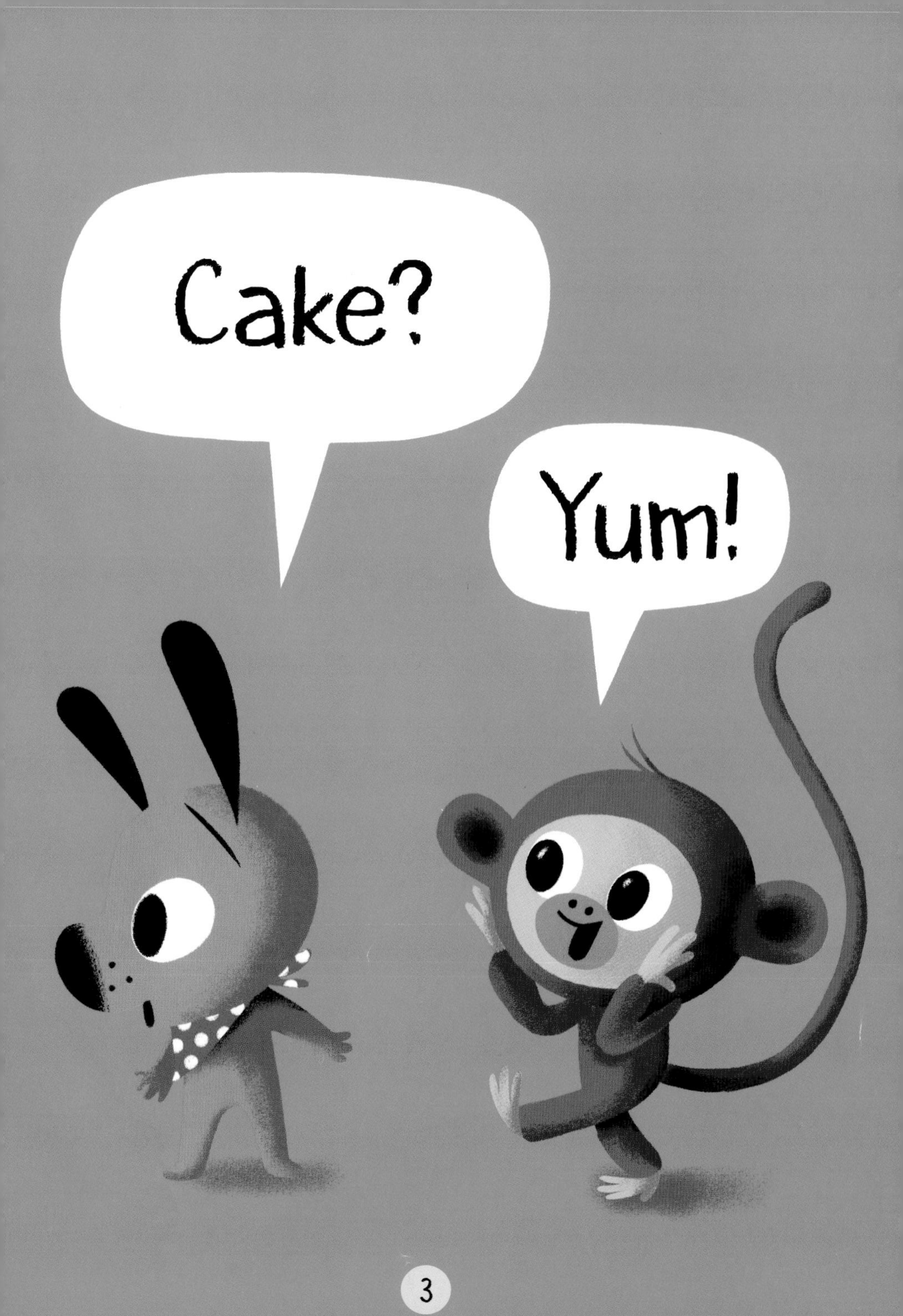
Cake?
Yum!

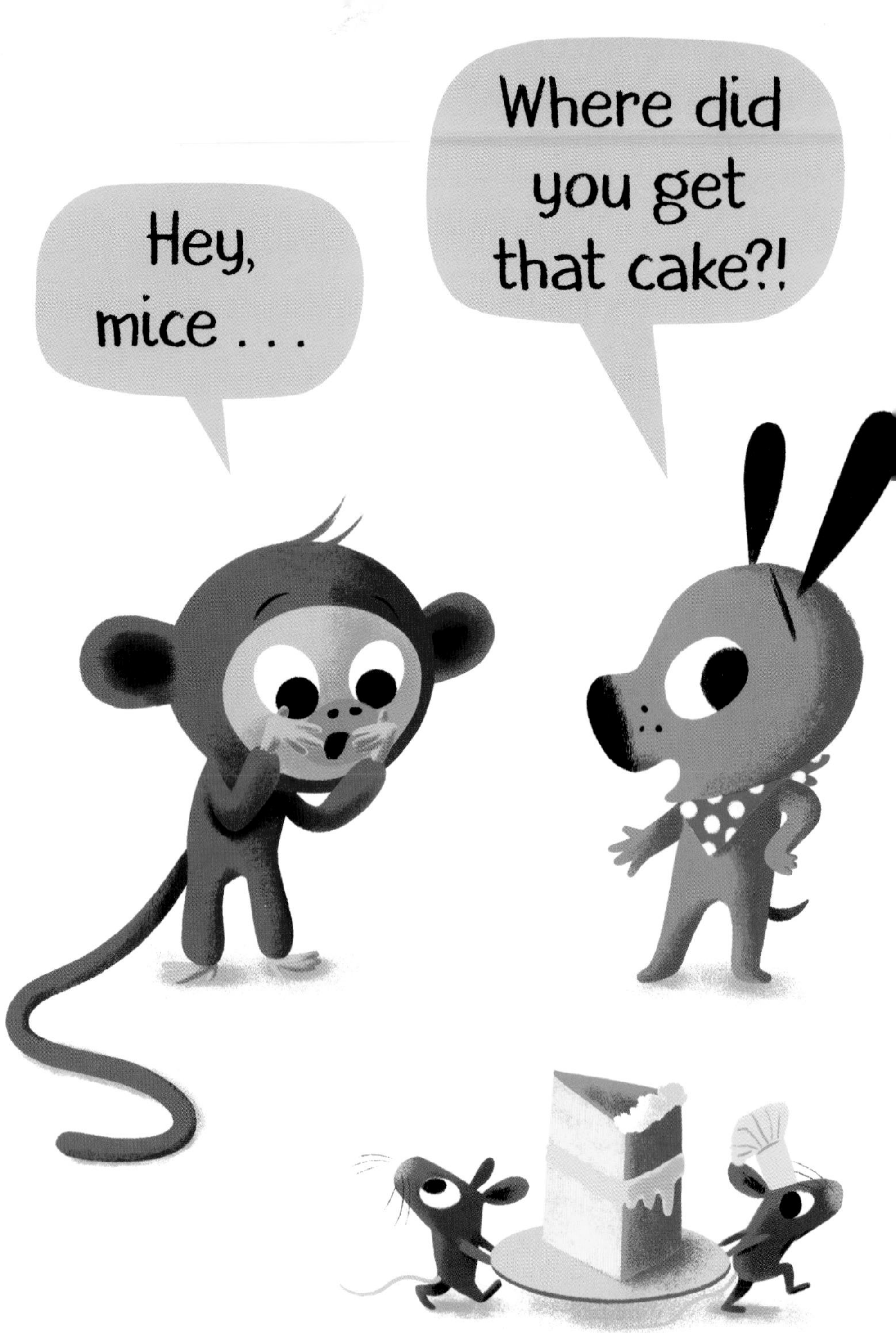
Hey, mice . . .
Where did you get that cake?!

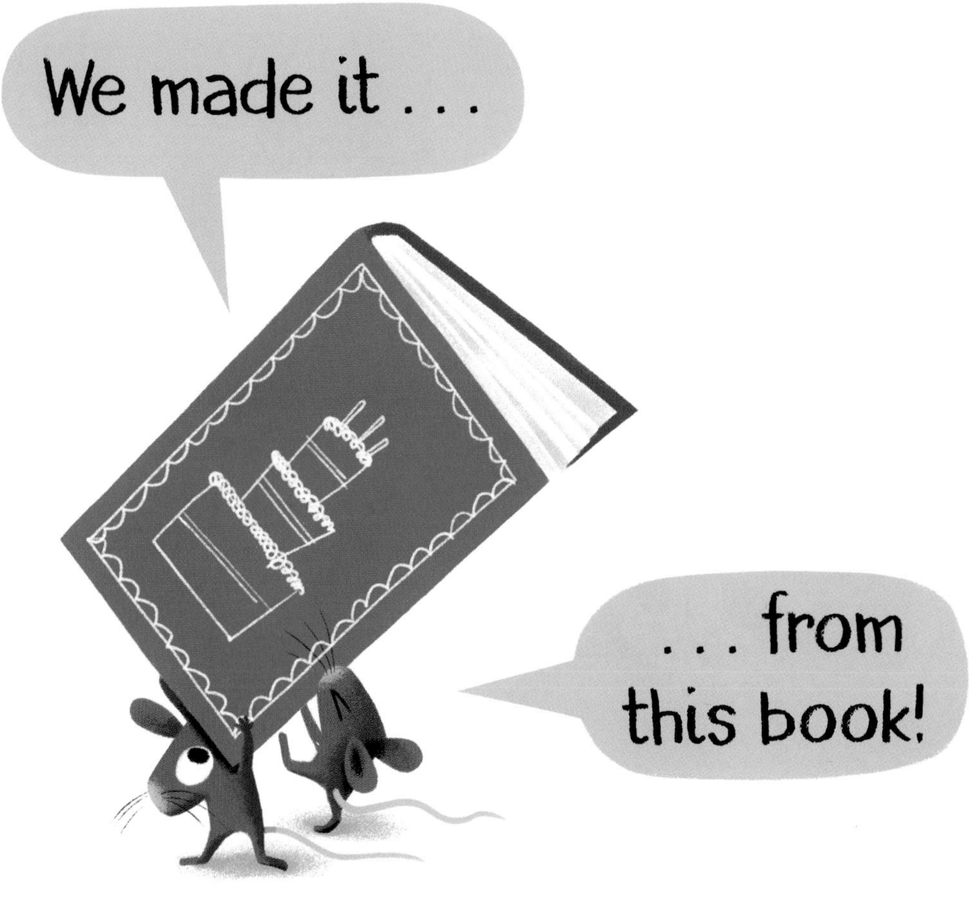
We made it . . .
. . . from this book!

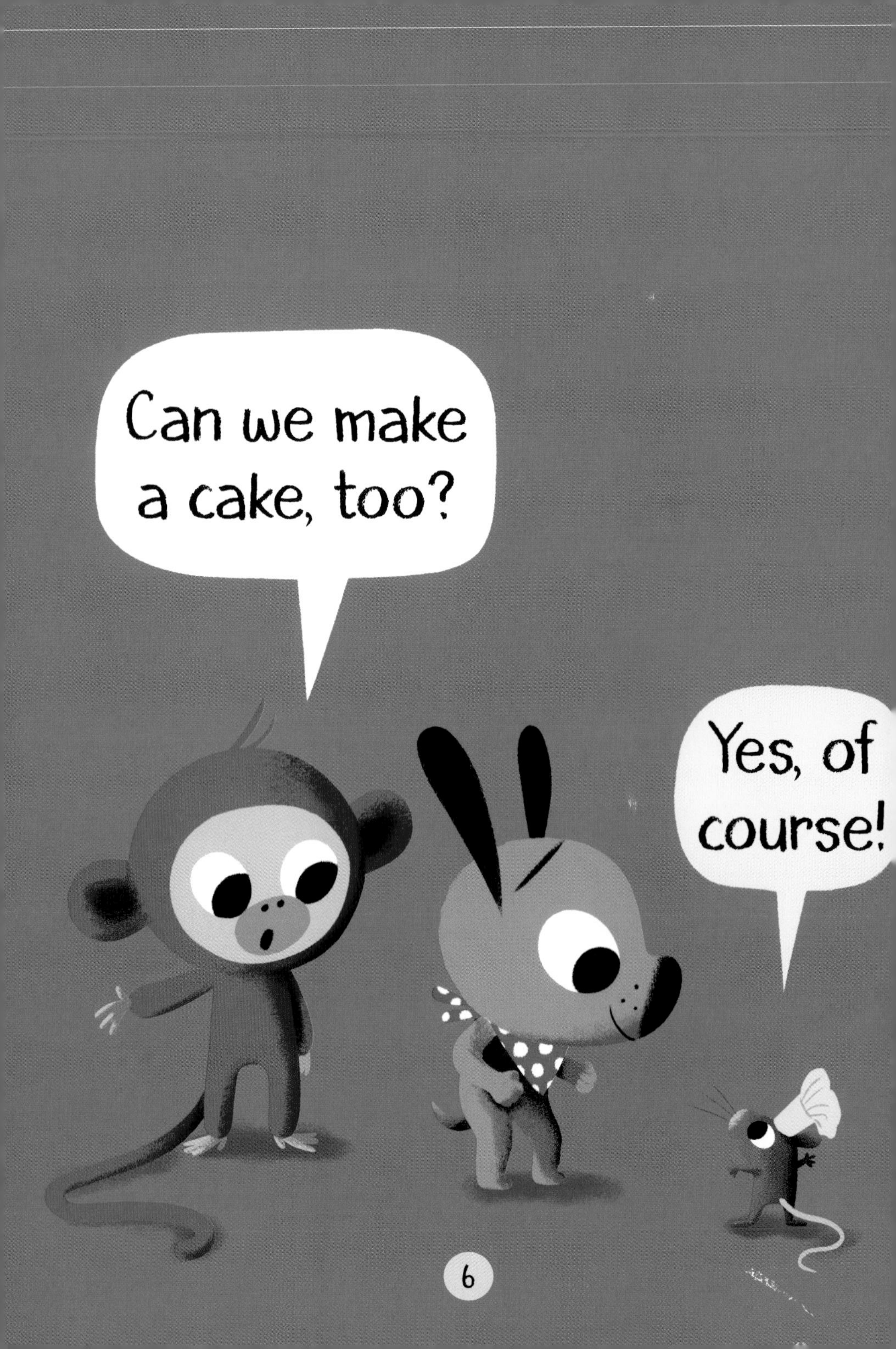
Can we make a cake, too?
Yes, of course!

Chapter 2
Make a Cake!

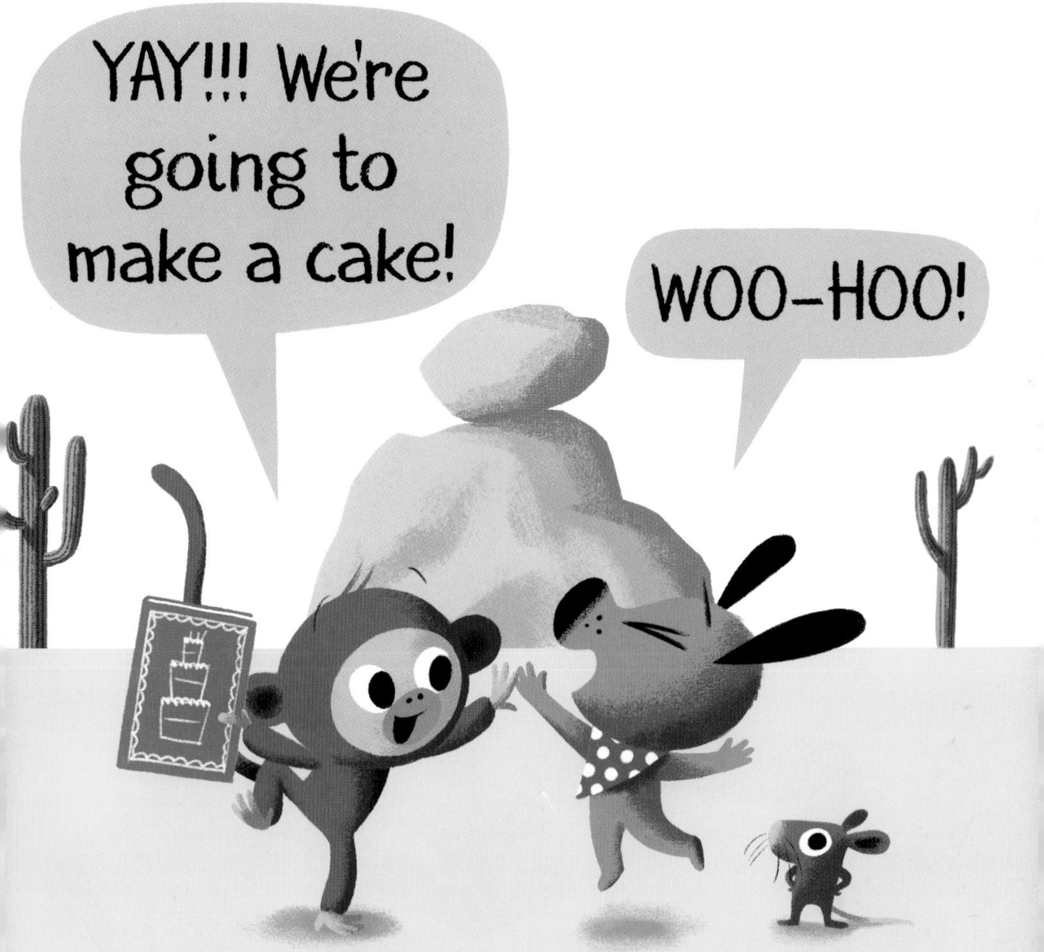
YAY!!! We're going to make a cake!
WOO-HOO!

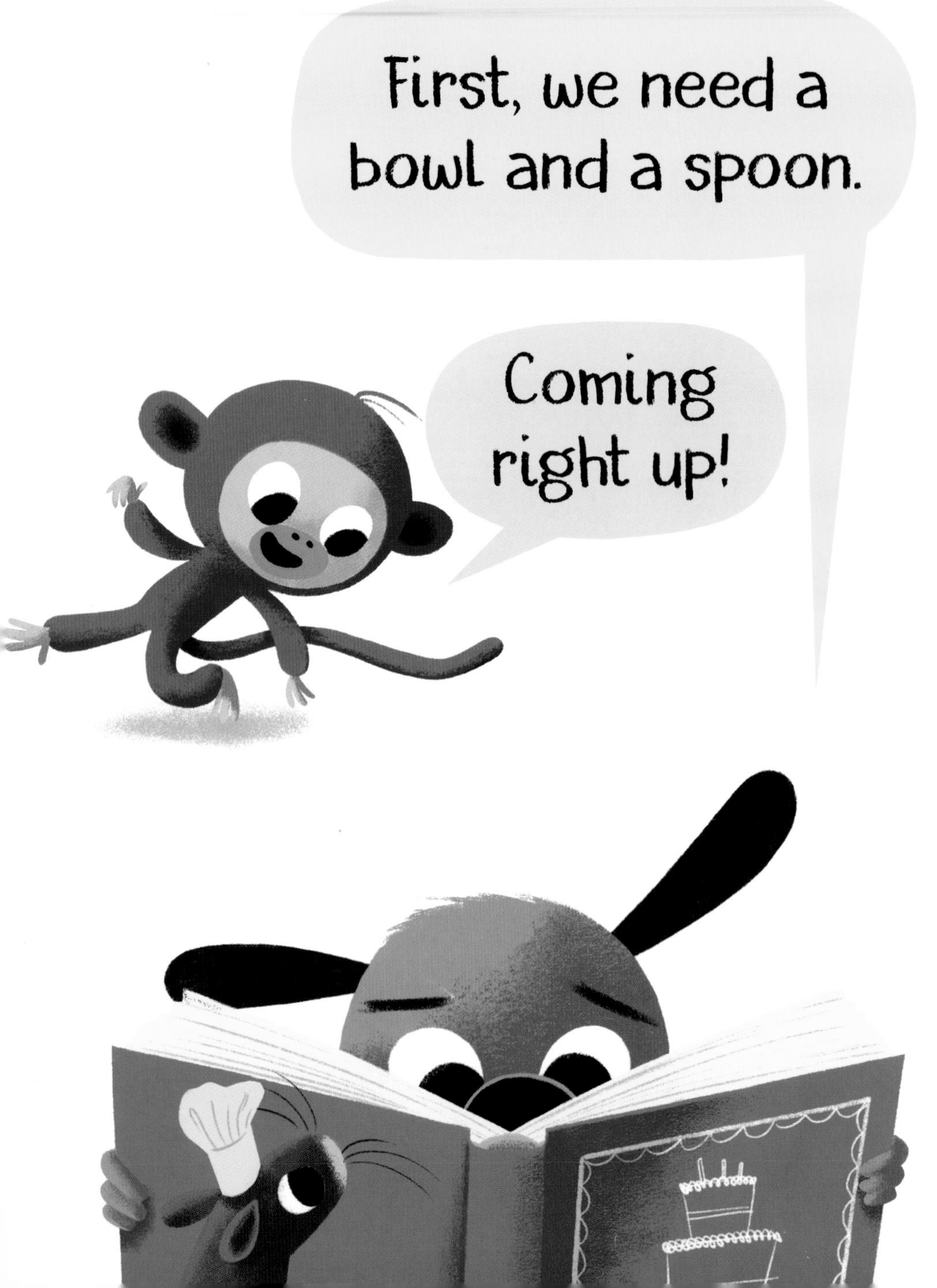
First, we need a bowl and a spoon.
Coming right up!

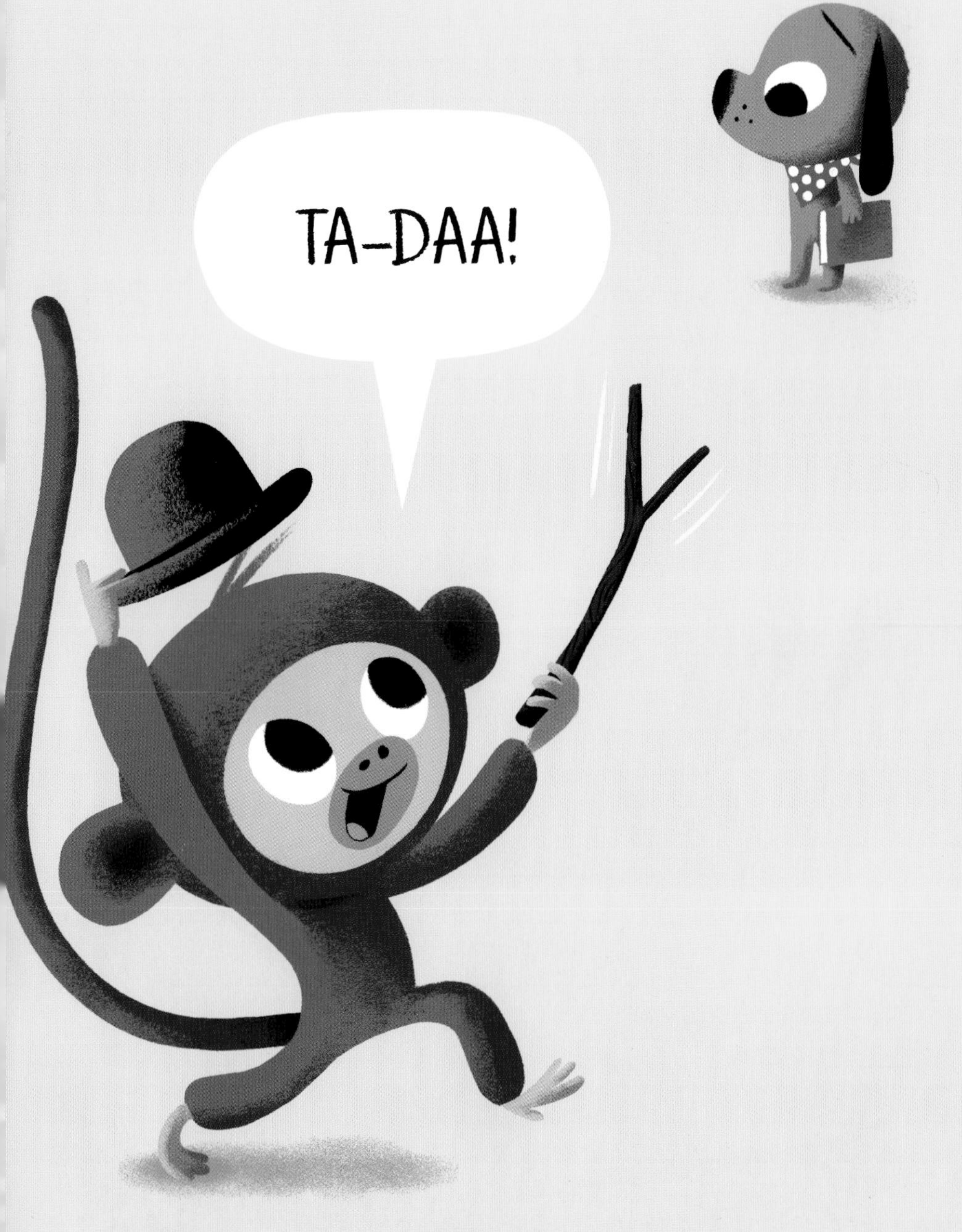
TA-DAA!

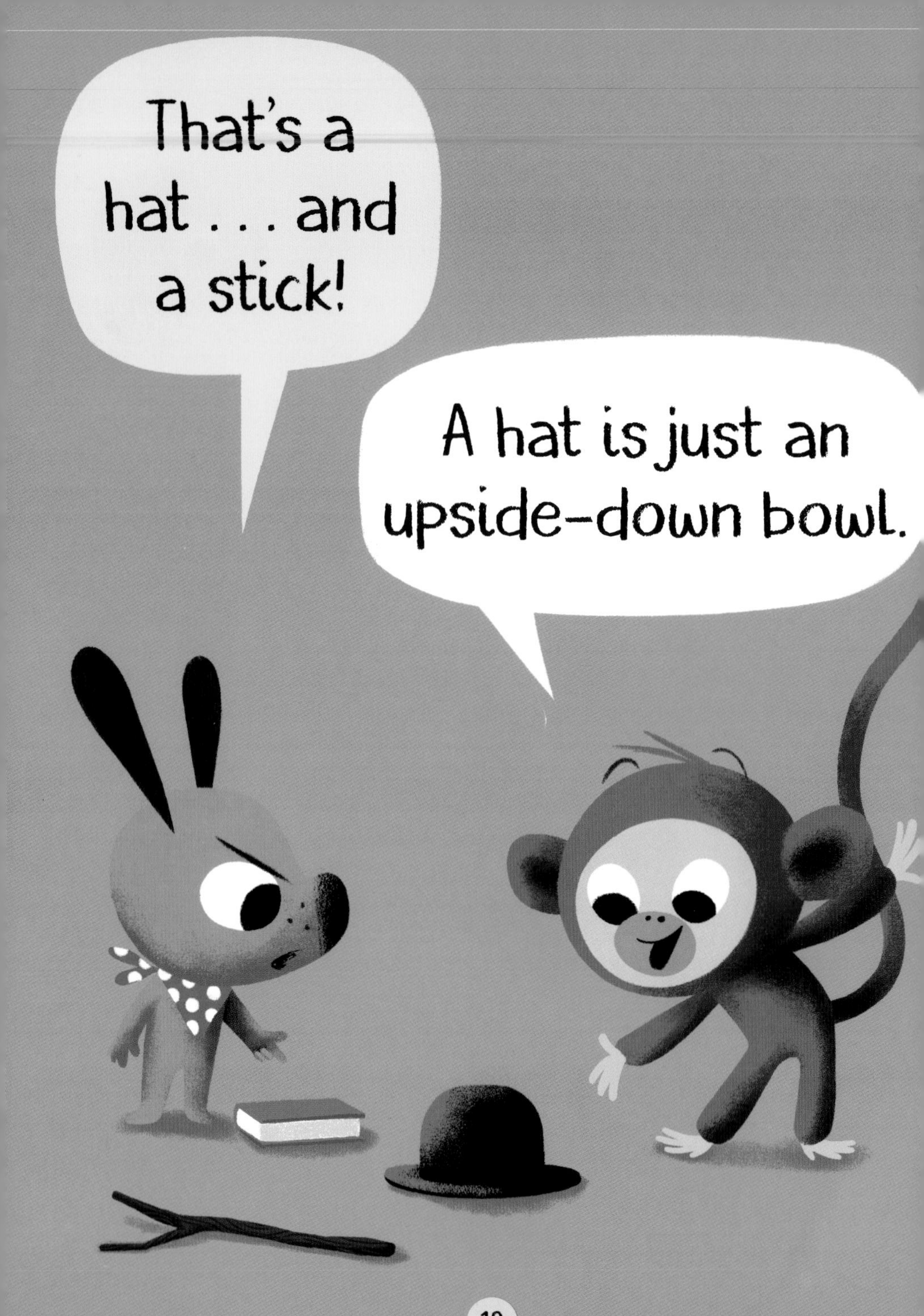
That's a hat . . . and a stick!
A hat is just an upside-down bowl.

A stick works
just like a spoon.

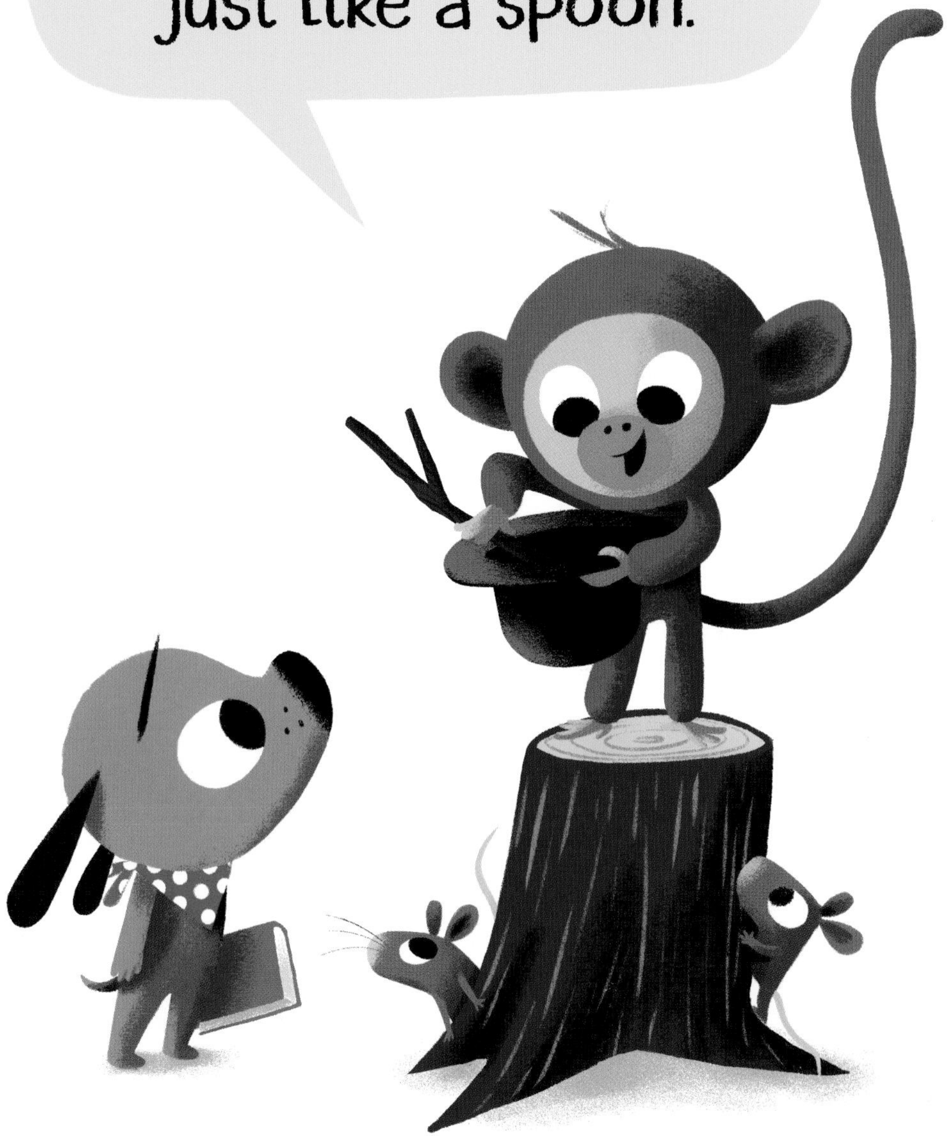

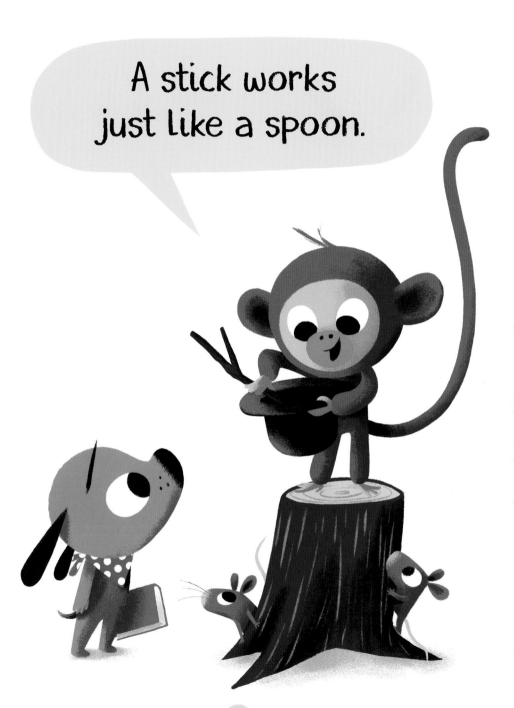

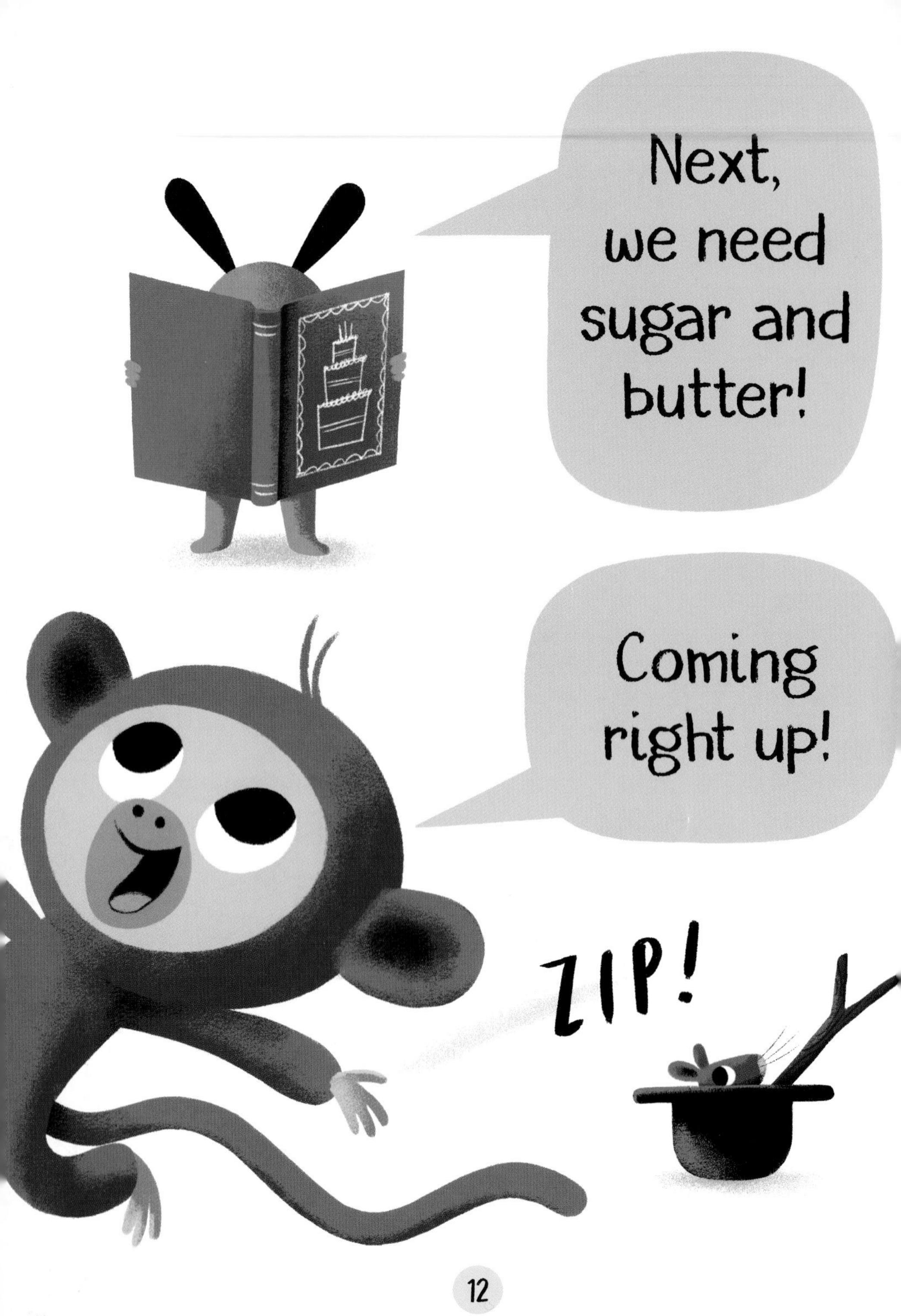
Next, we need sugar and butter!
Coming right up!
ZIP!

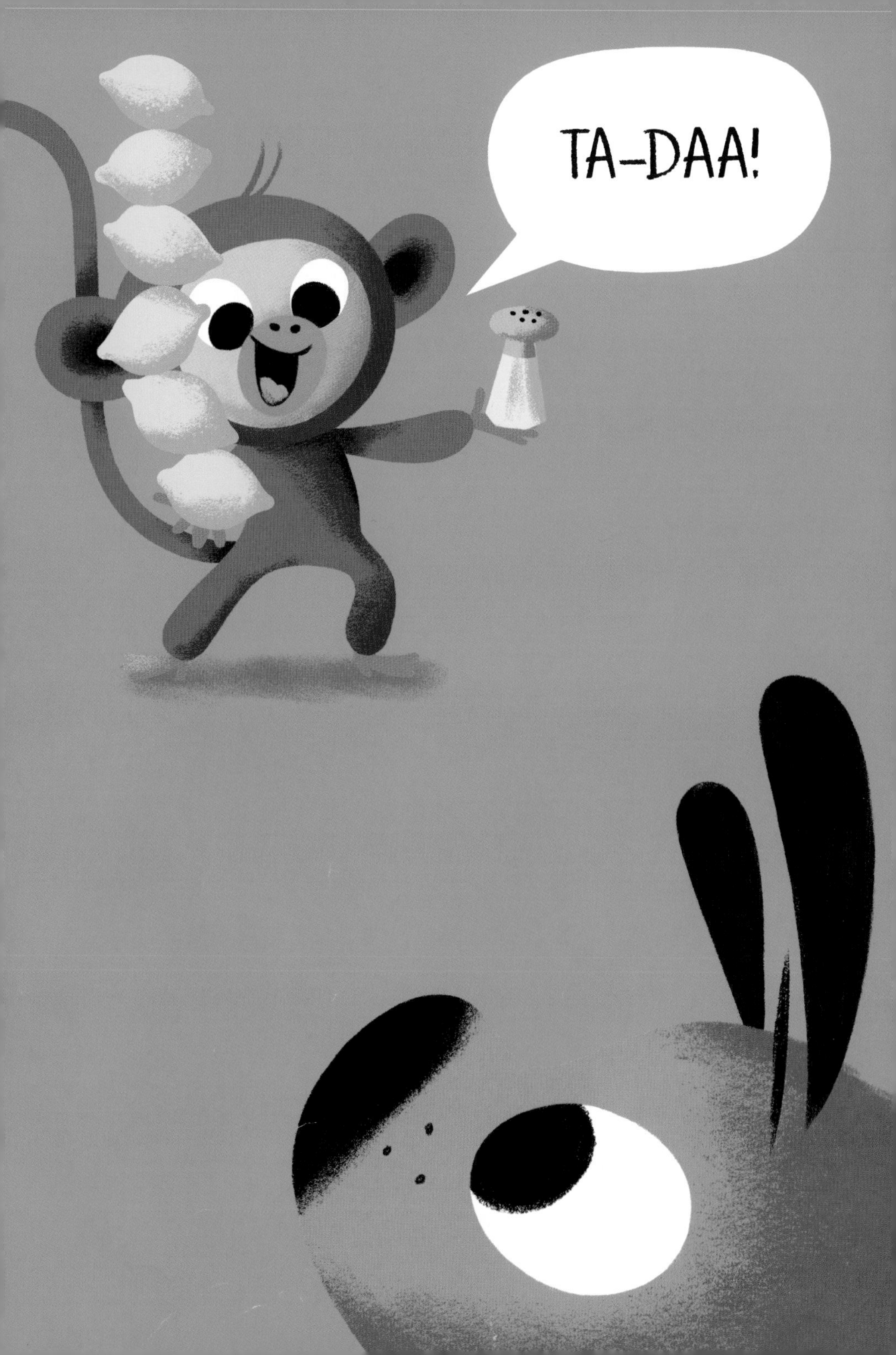
TA-DAA!

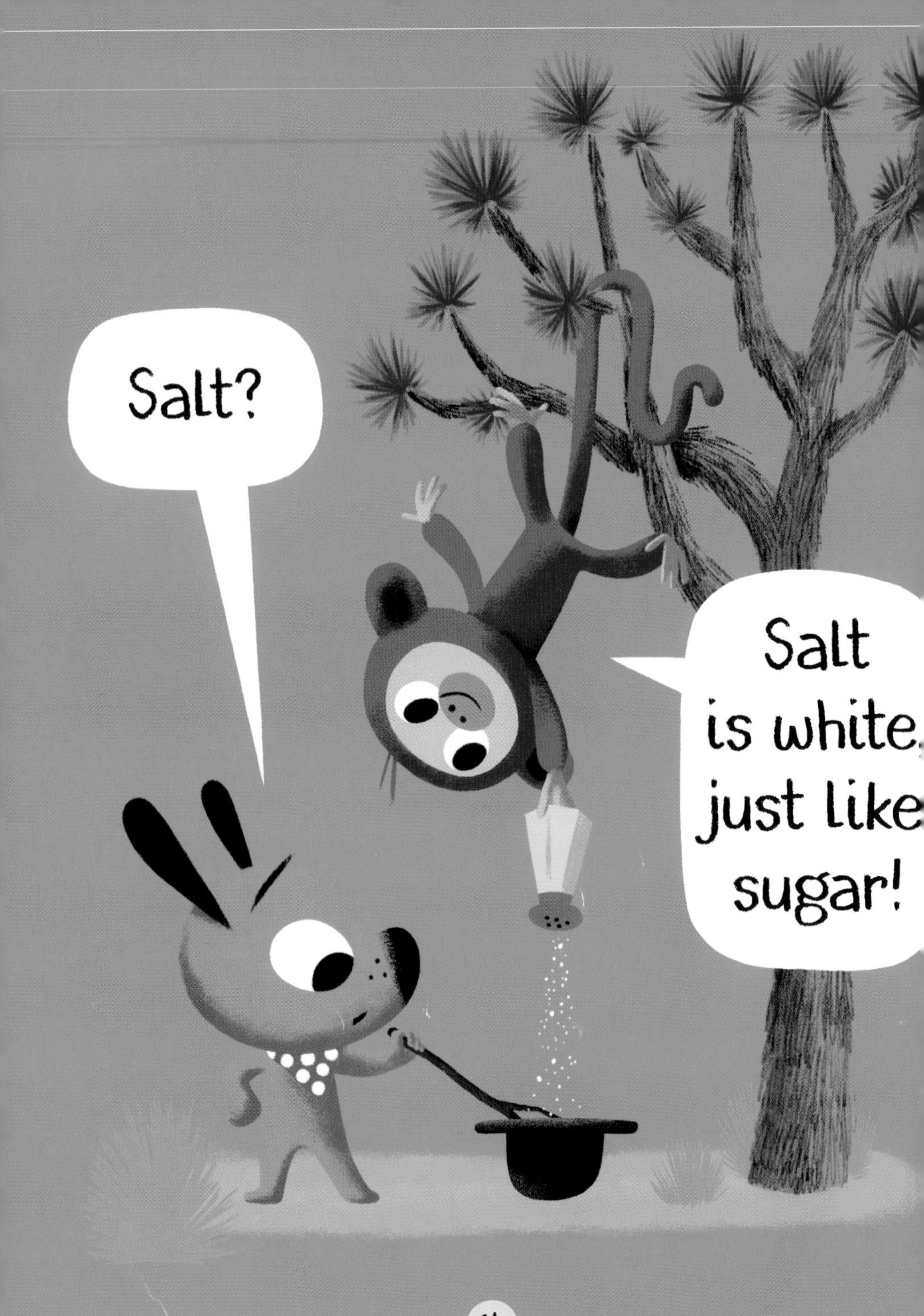
Salt?
Salt is white, just like sugar!

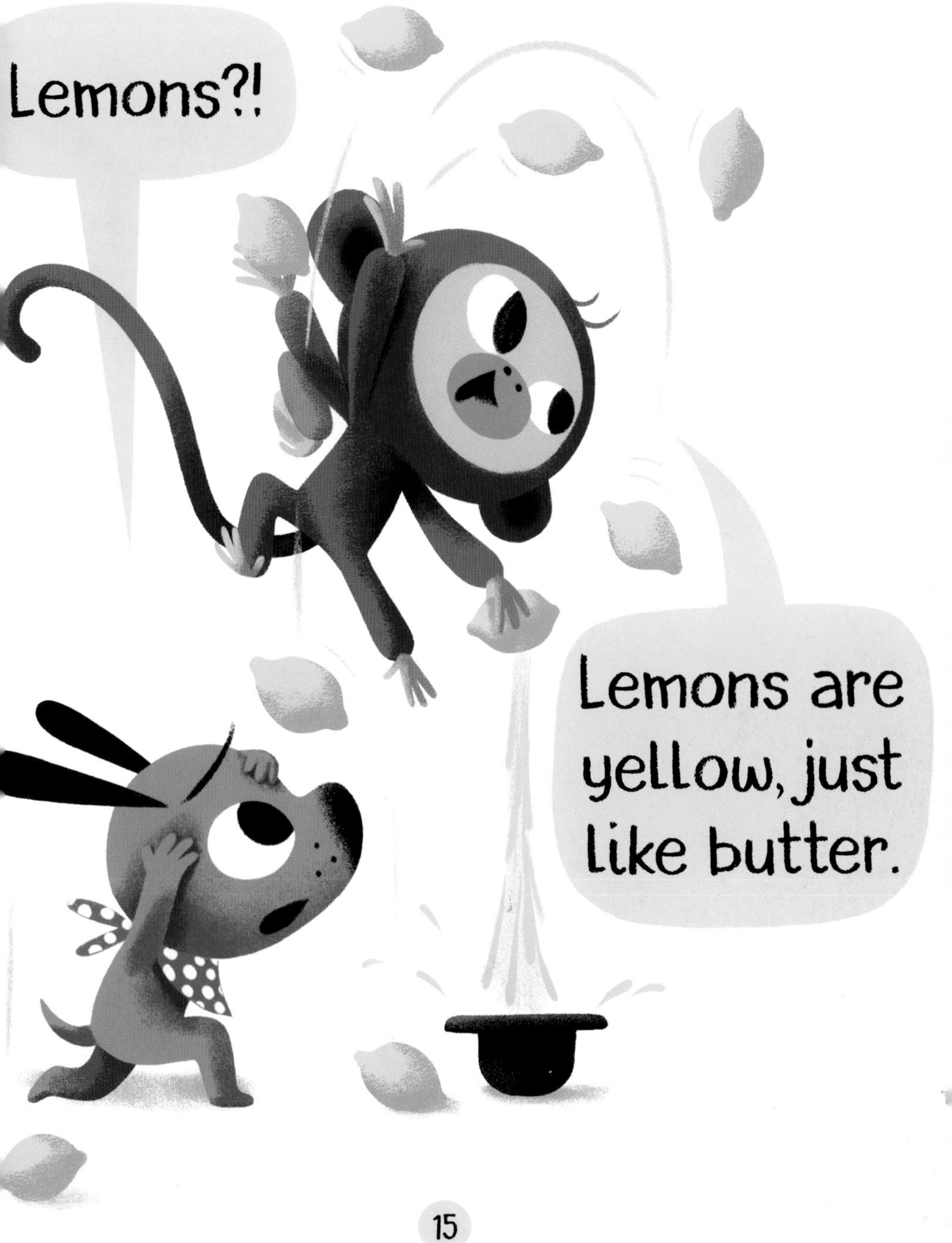
Lemons?!
Lemons are yellow, just like butter.

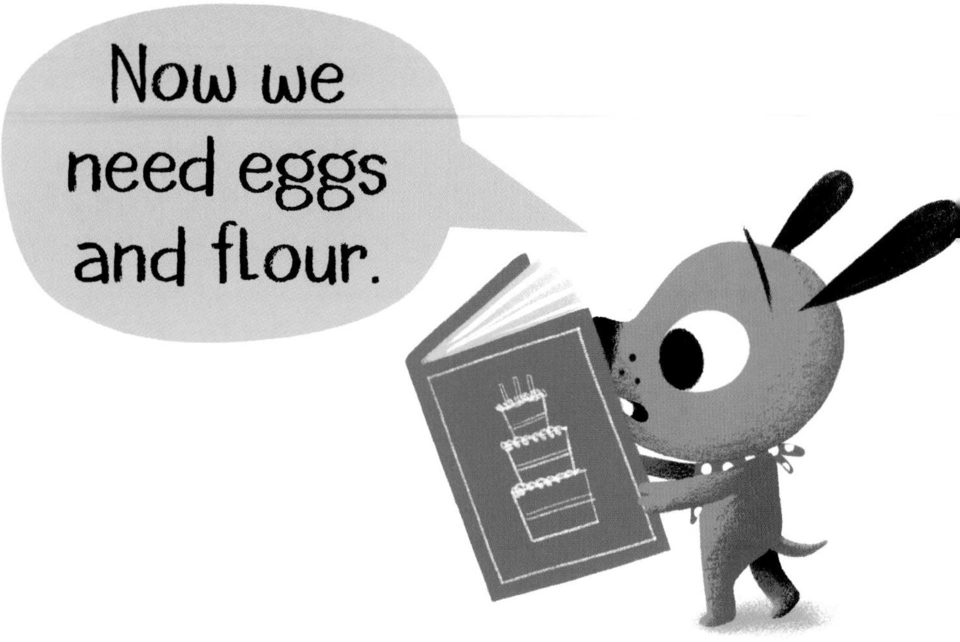
Now we
need eggs
and flour.

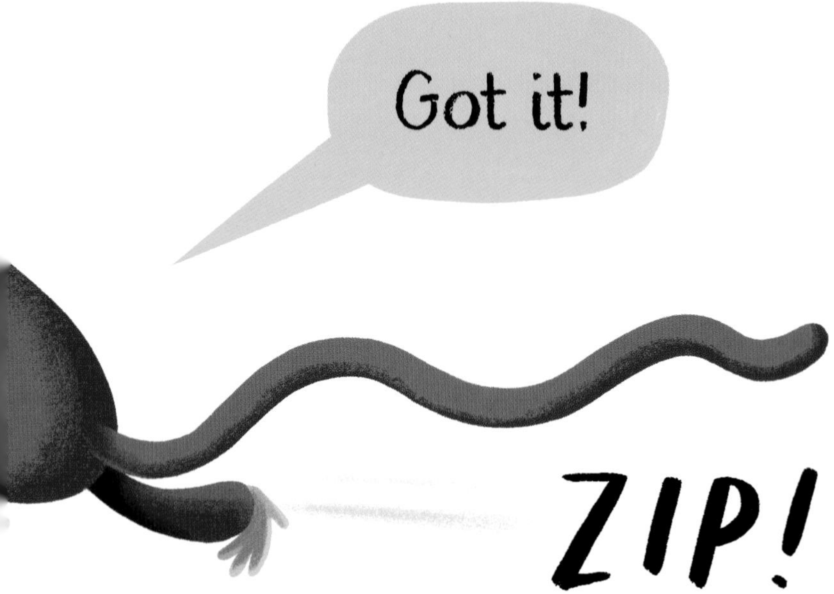
Got it!
ZIP!

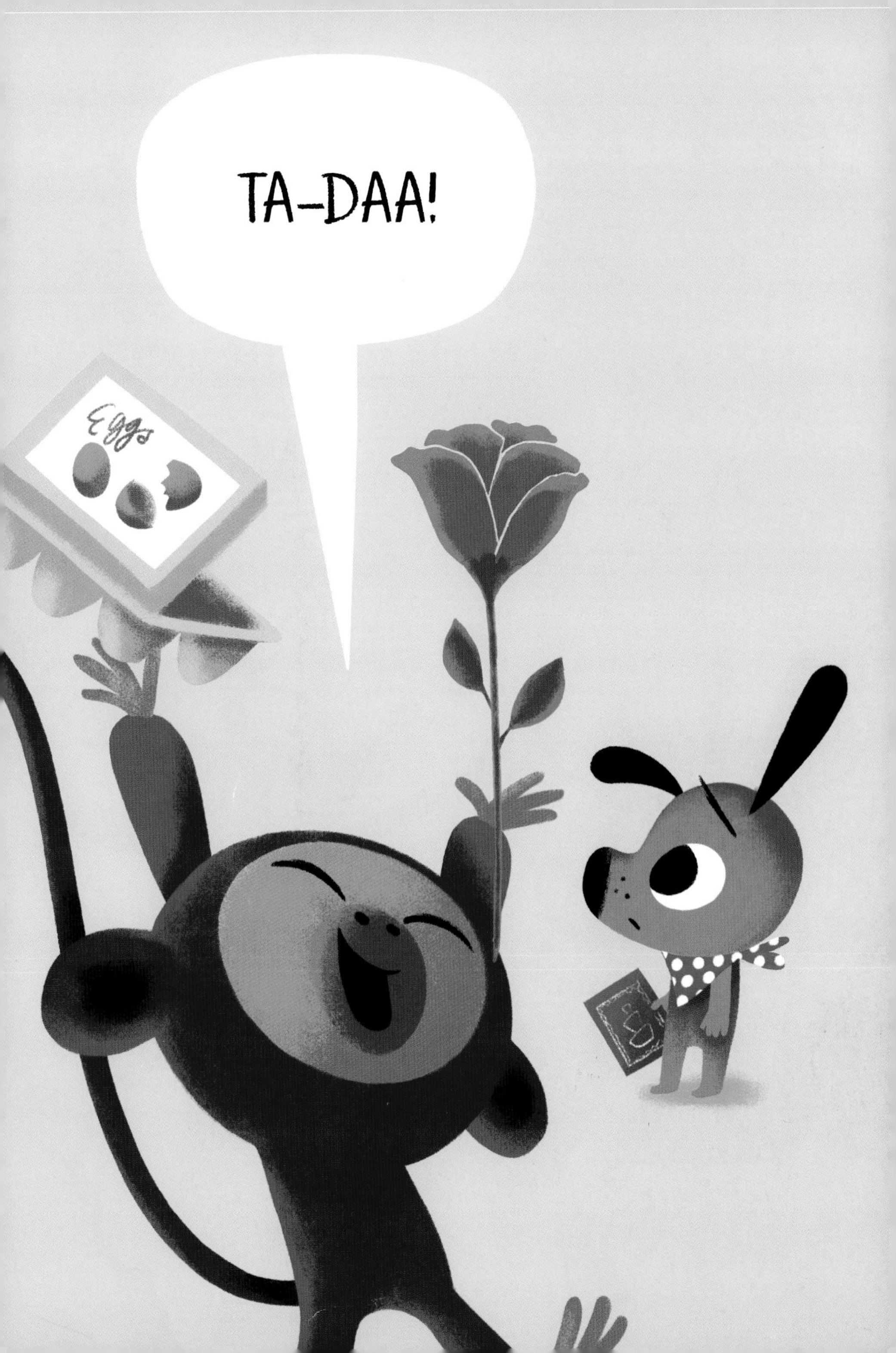
TA-DAA!
Eggs

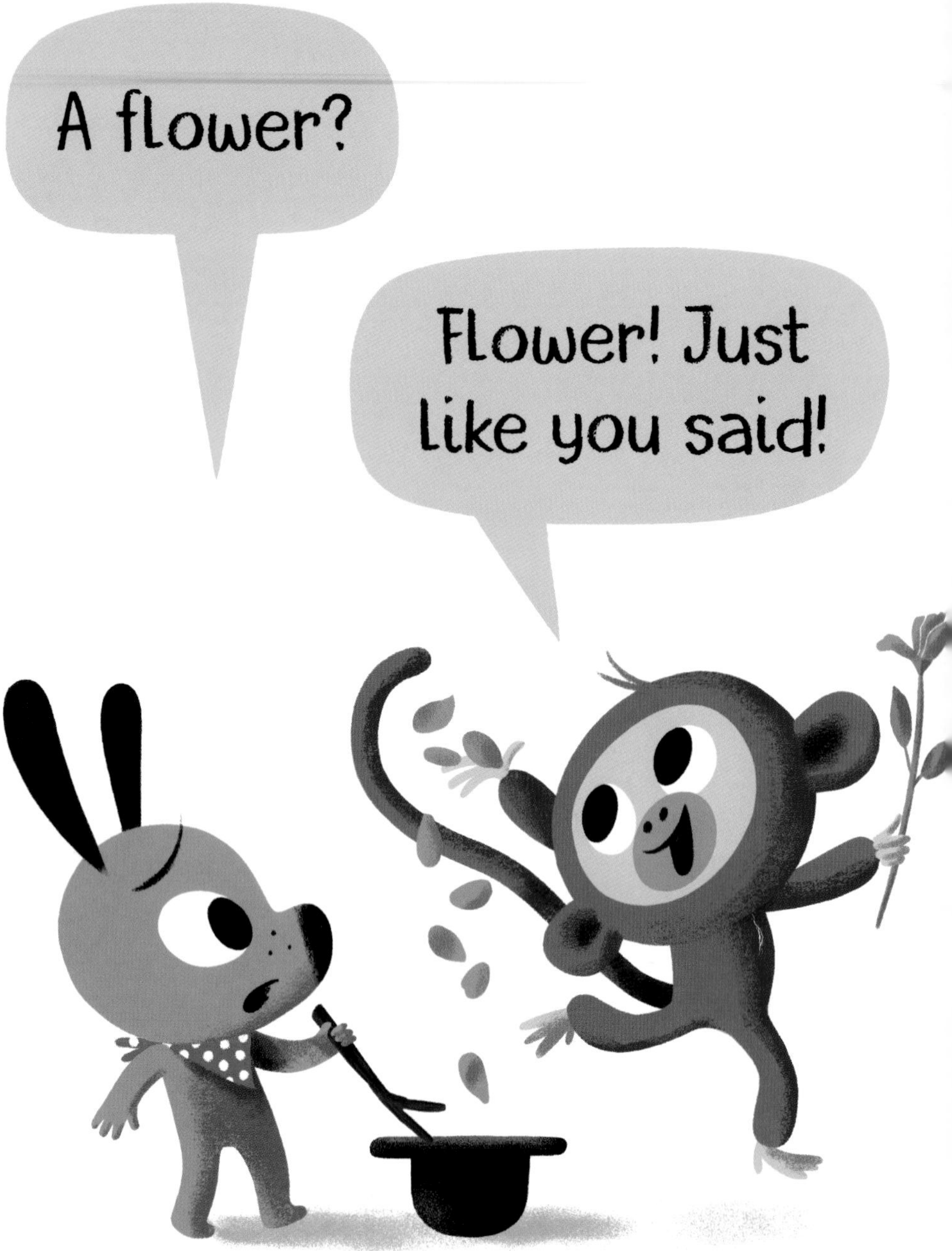
A flower?
Flower! Just like you said!

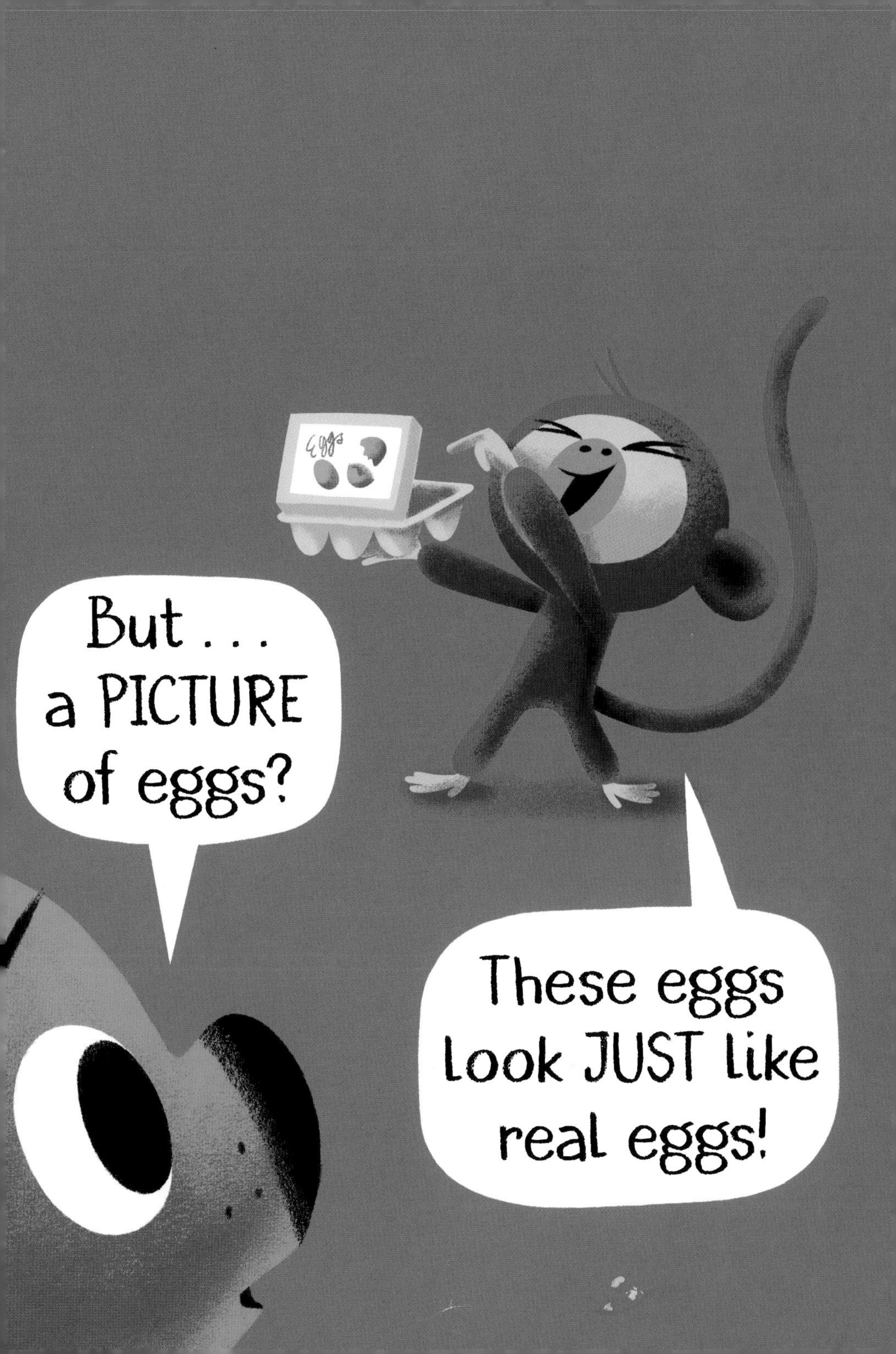
Eggs
But . . . a PICTURE of eggs?
These eggs look JUST like real eggs!

Chapter 3
Hot-Spot Cake

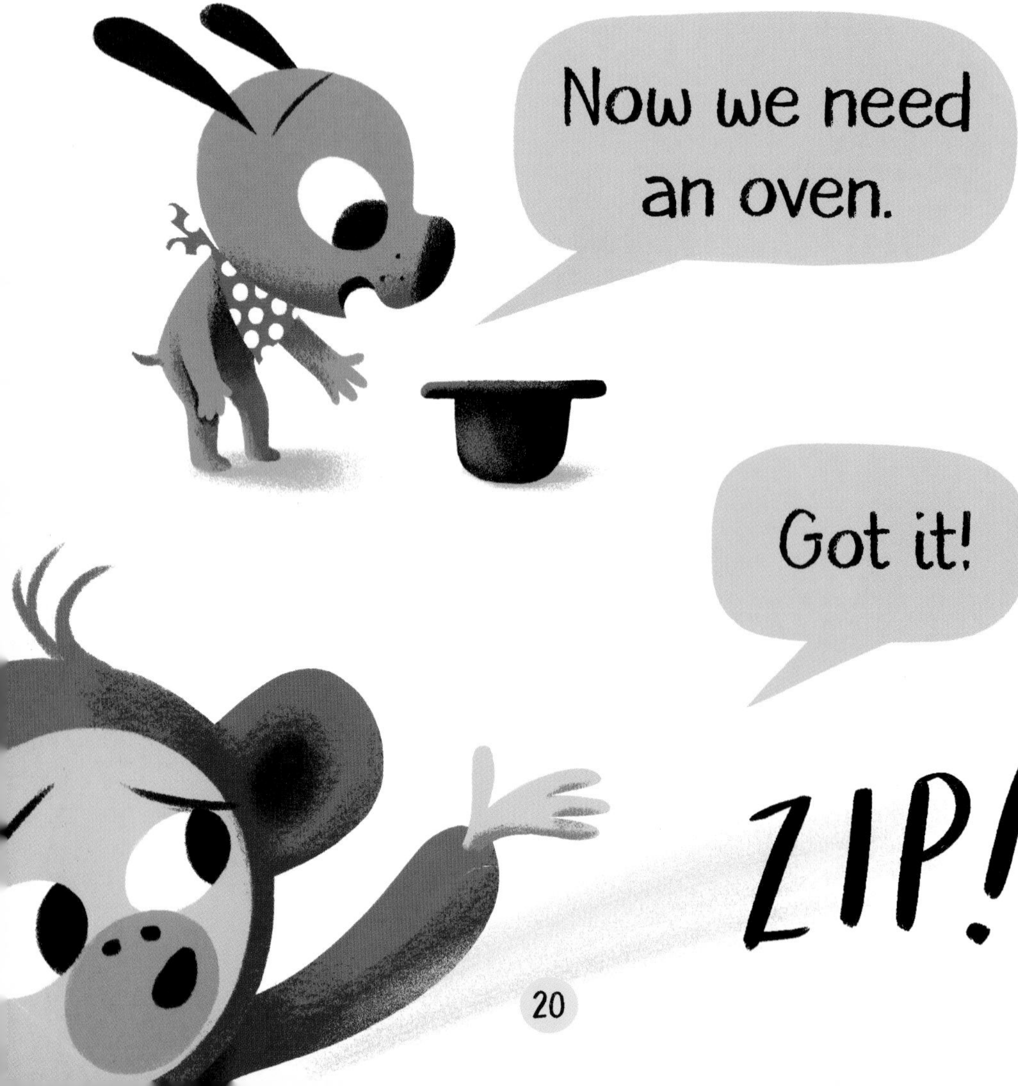
Now we need an oven.
Got it!
ZIP!

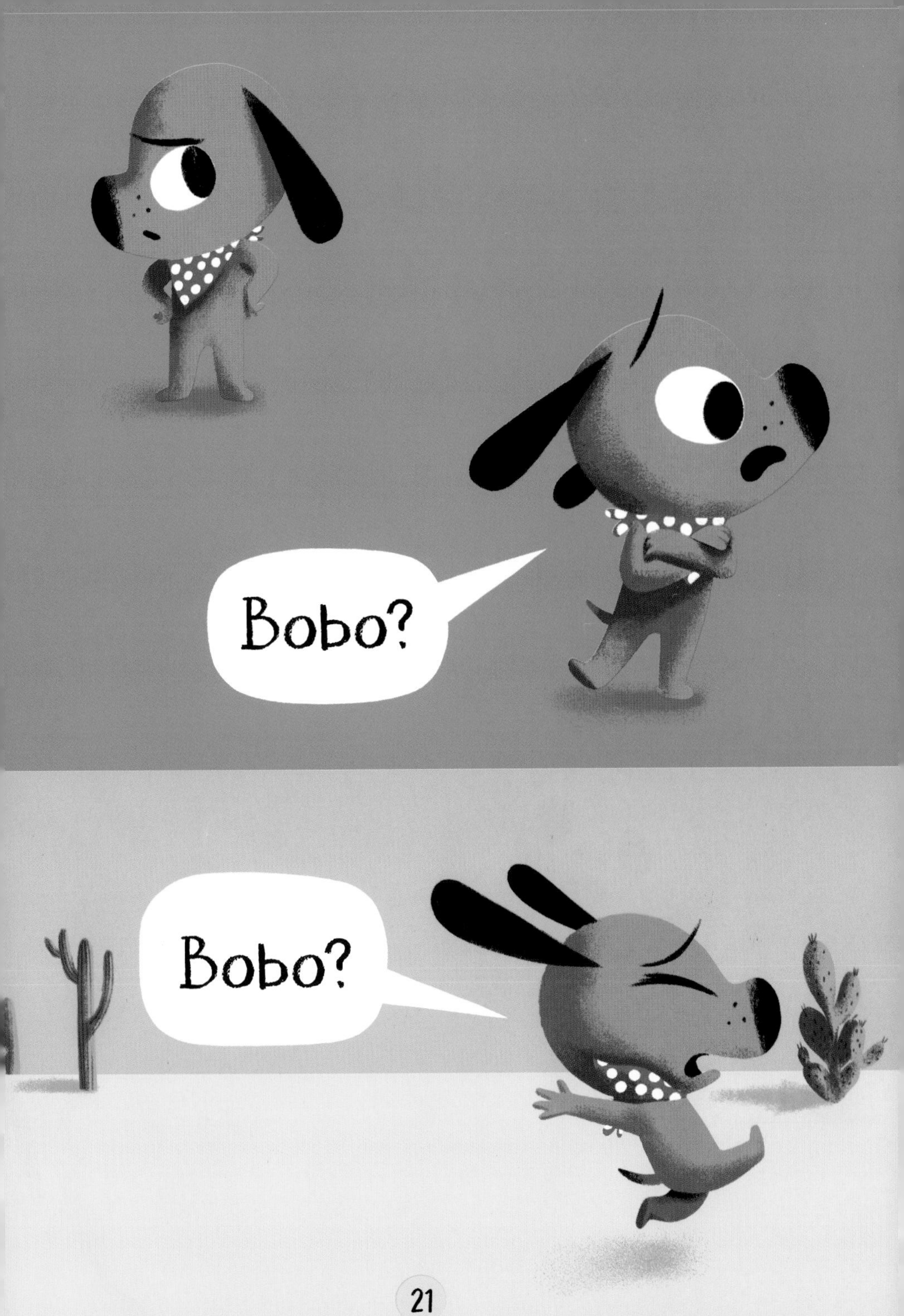
Bobo?
Bobo?

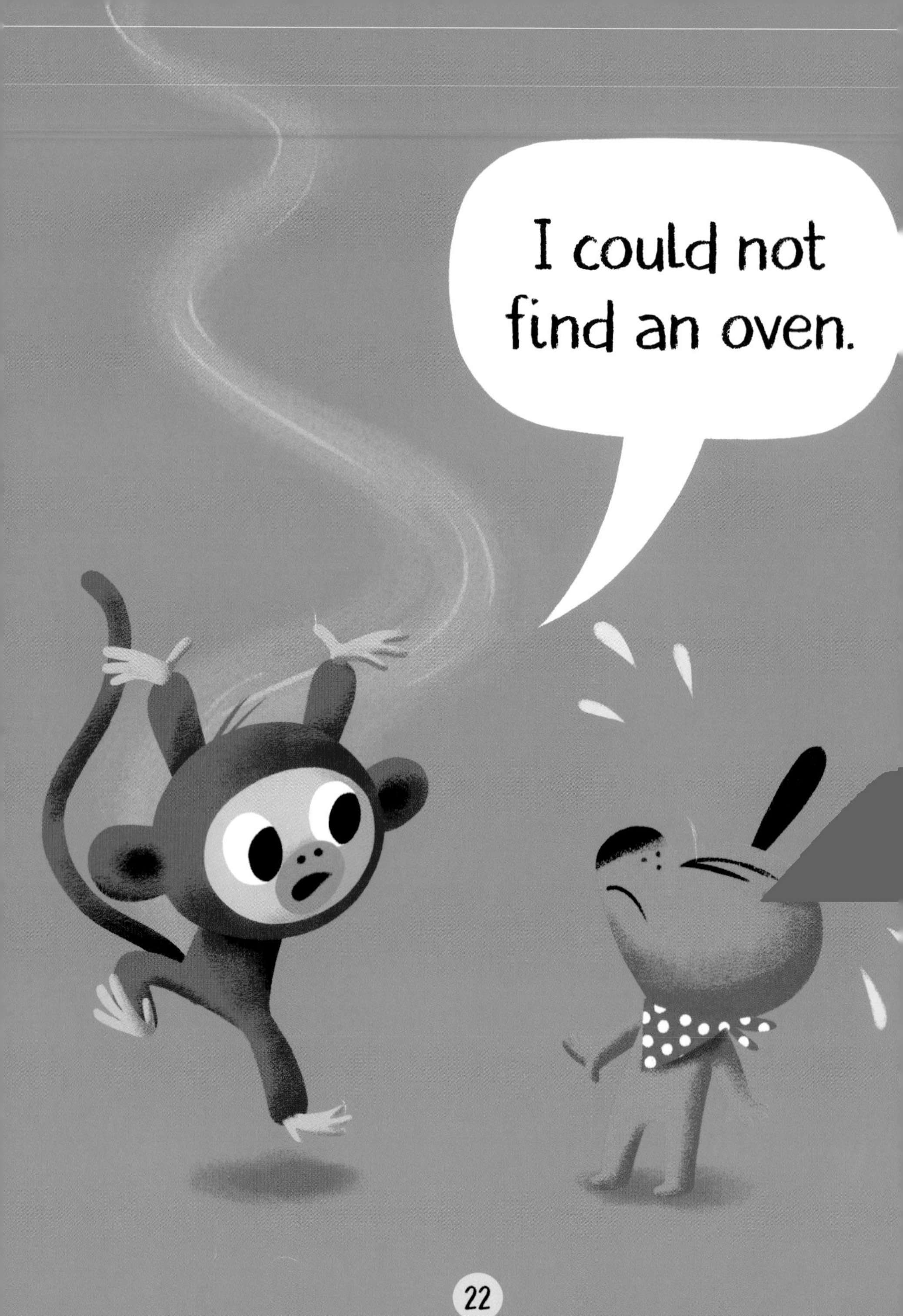
I could not find an oven.

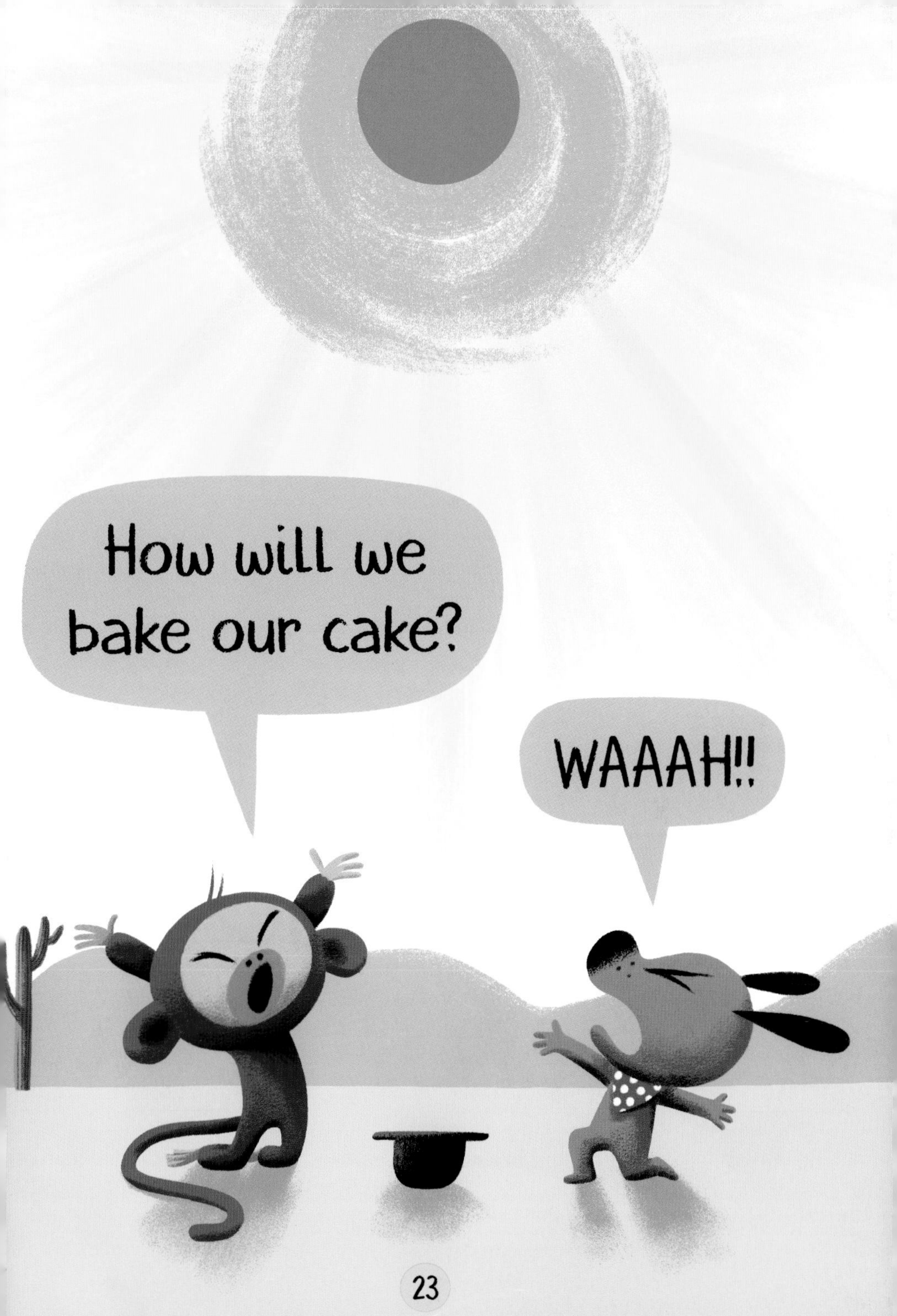
How will we bake our cake?
WAAAH!!

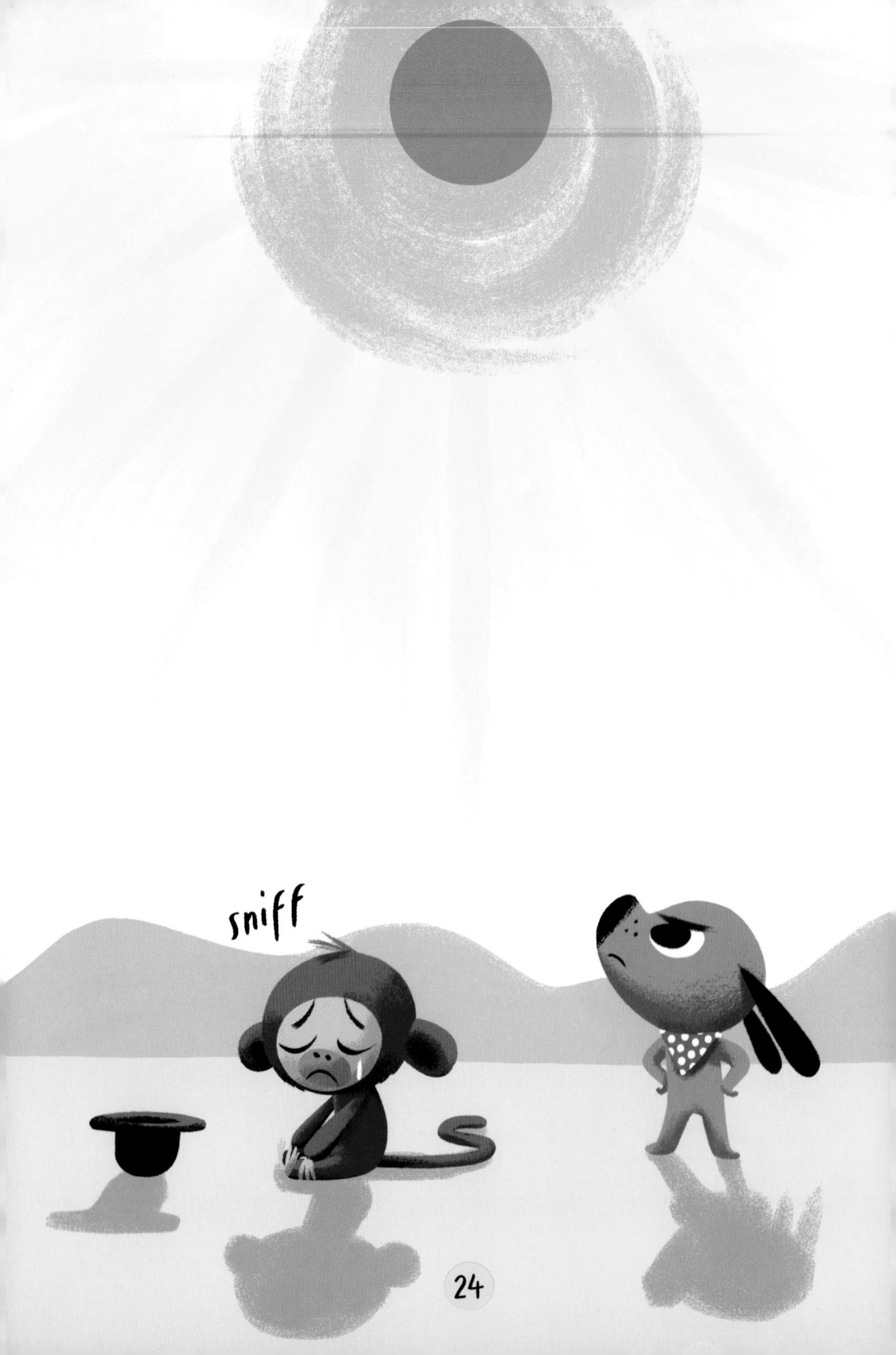
sniff

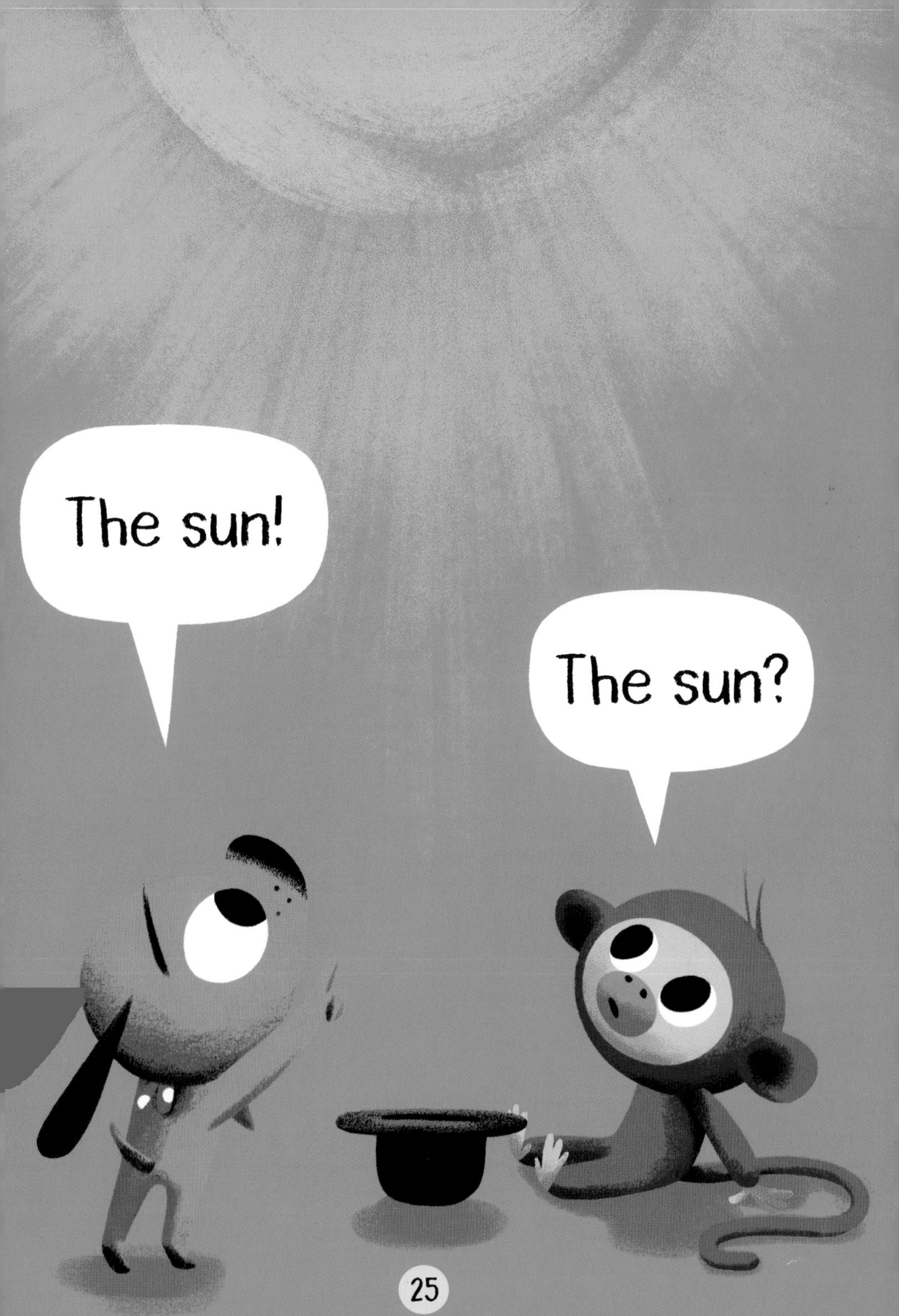
The sun!
The sun?

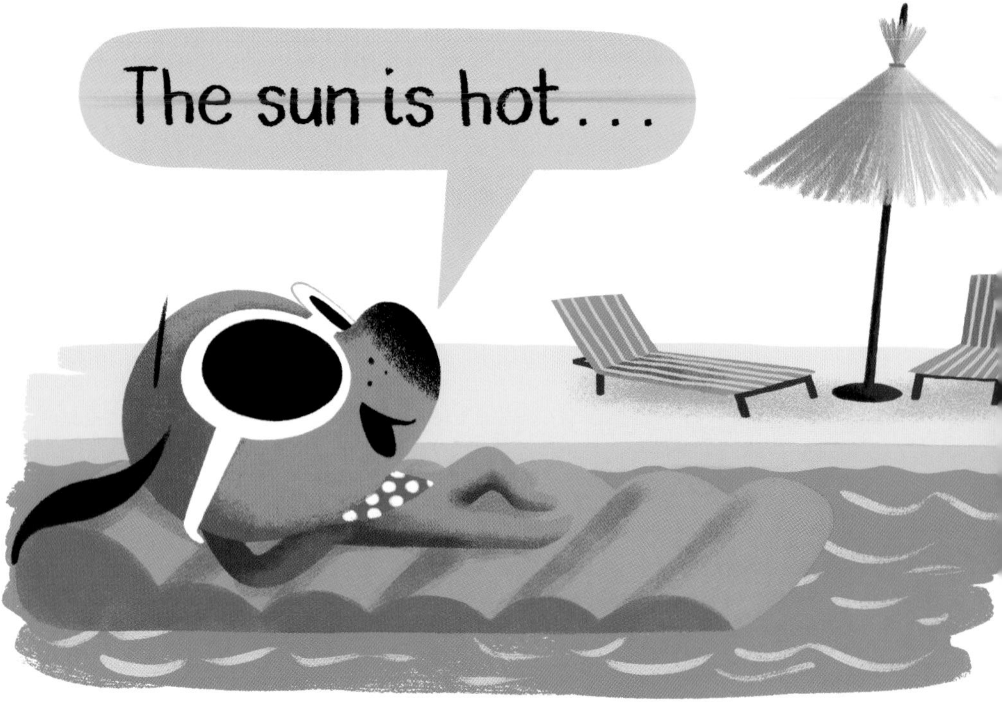
The sun is hot . . .

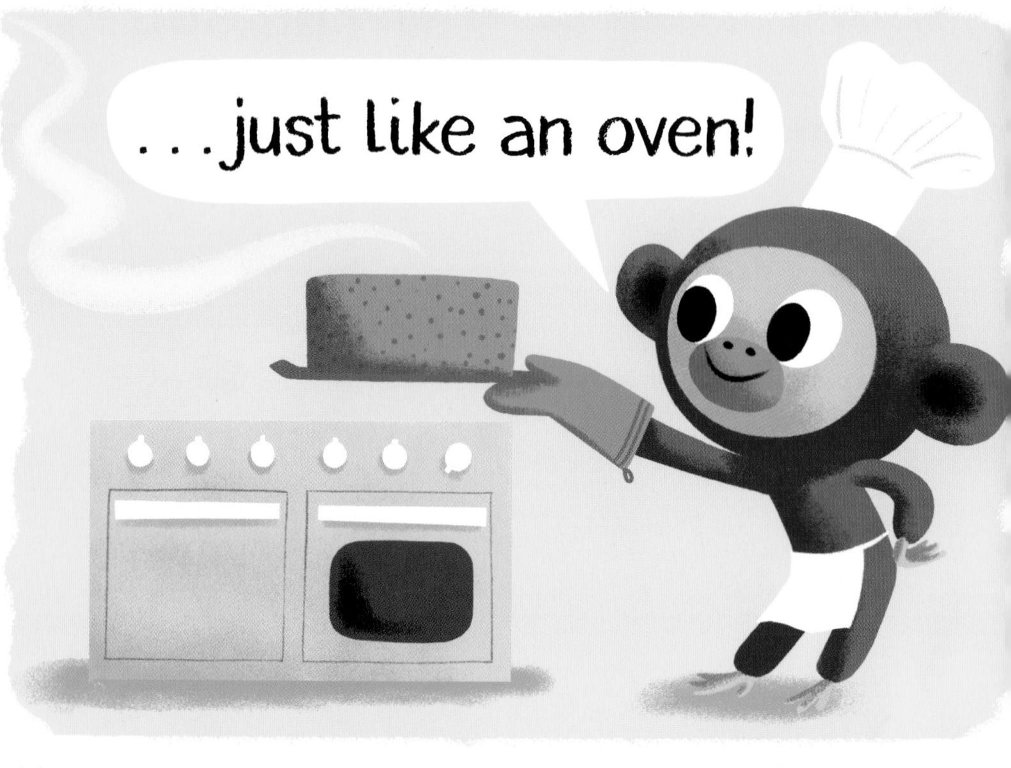
. . . just like an oven!

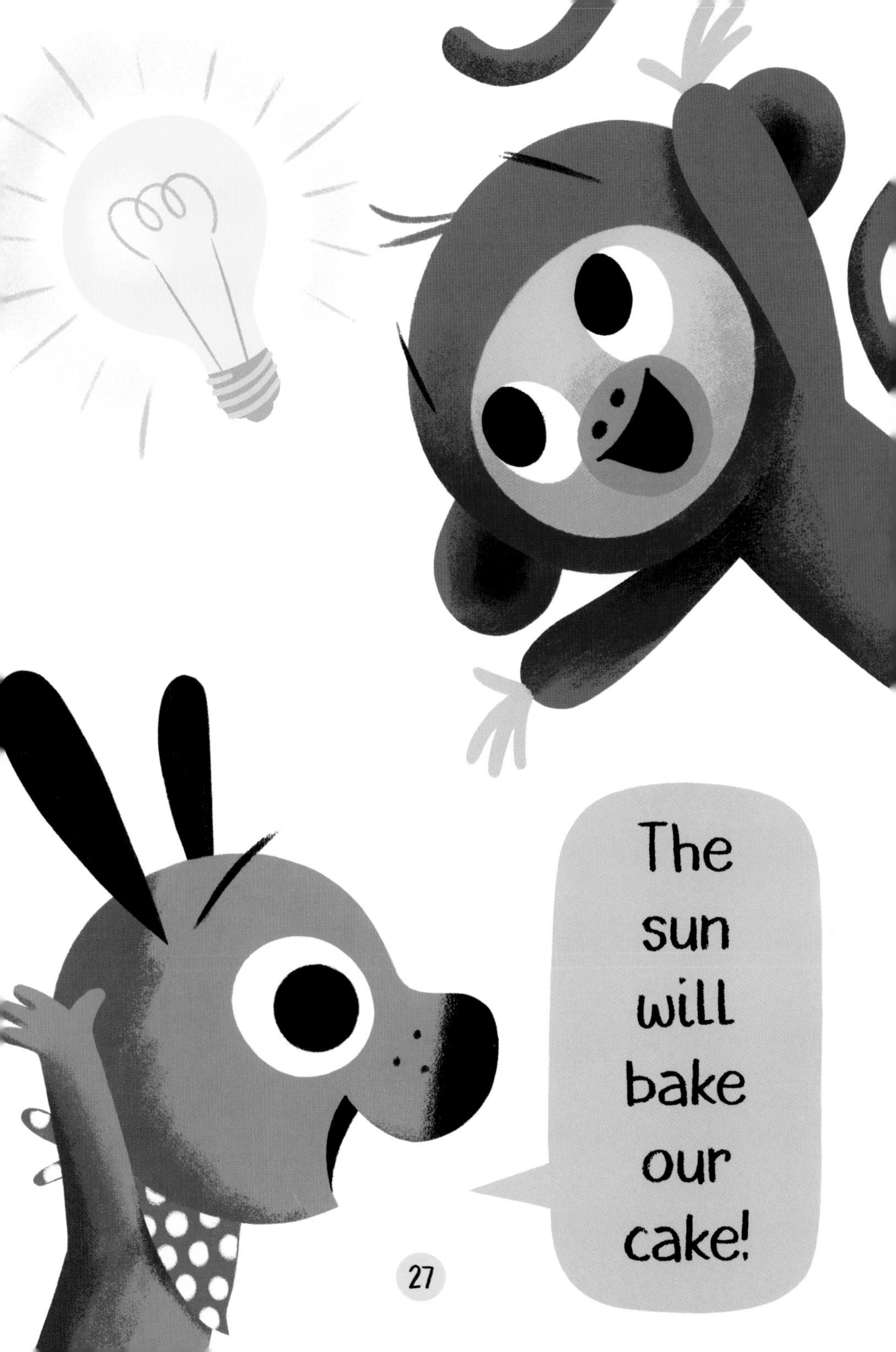
The sun will bake our cake!

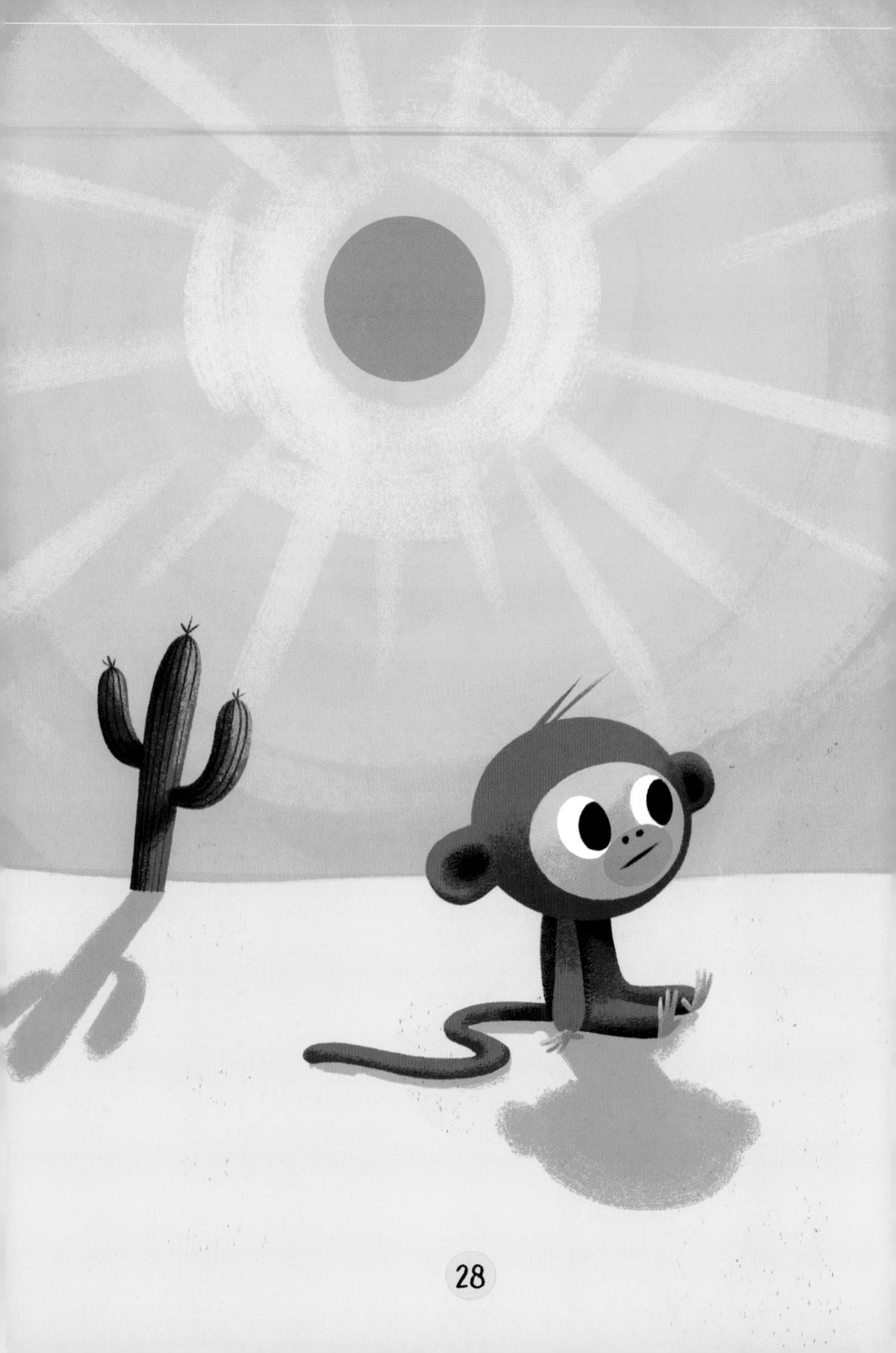

Chapter 4
Bake, Cake, Bake!

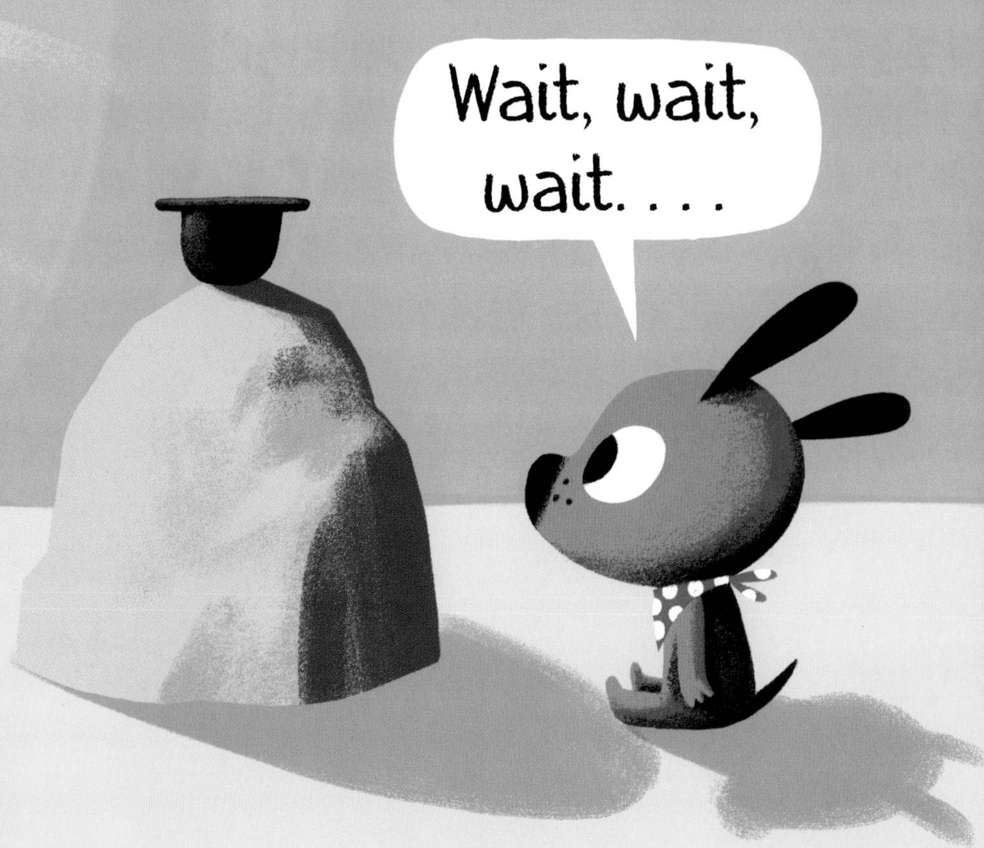
Wait, wait,
wait. . . .

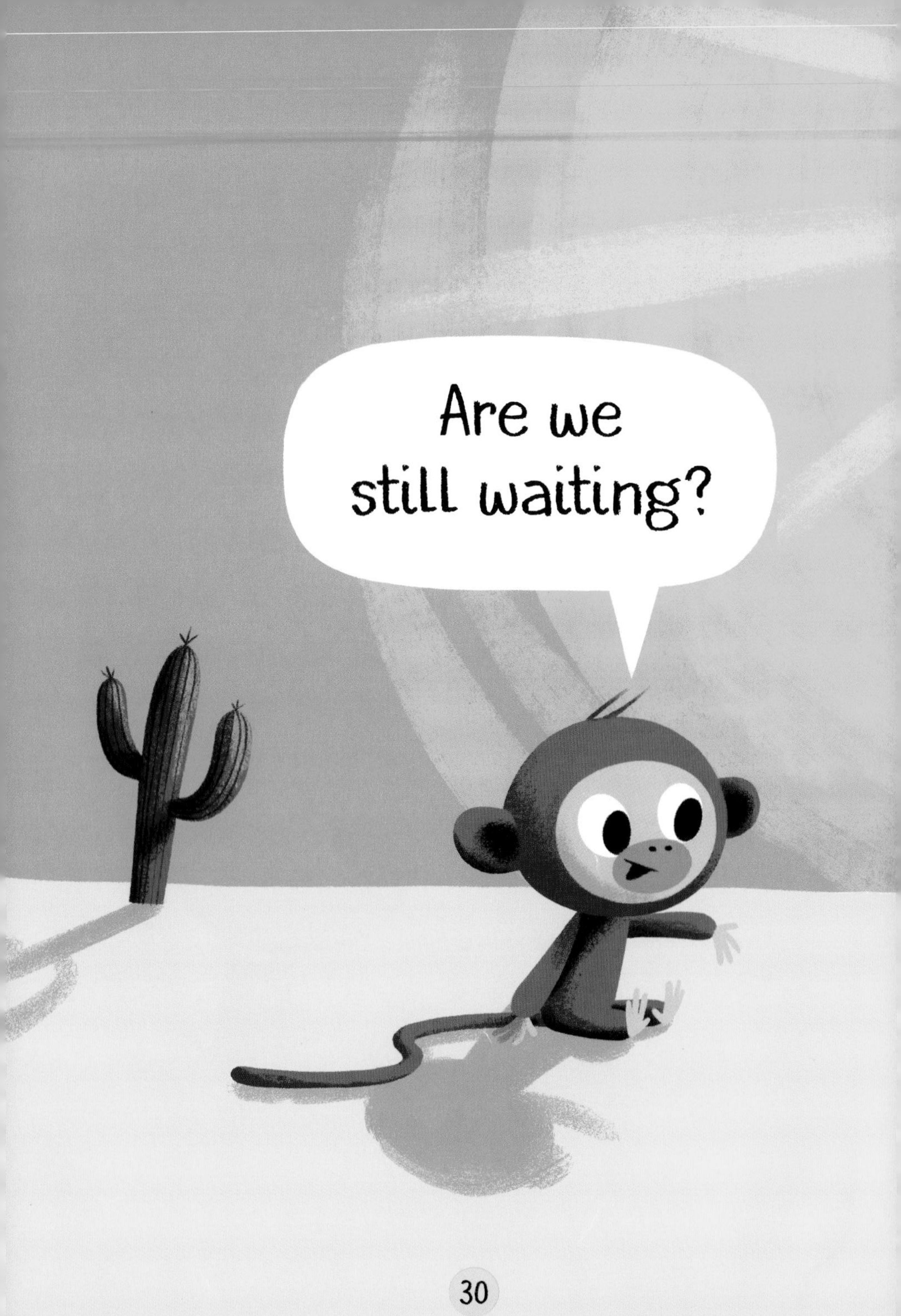
Are we
still waiting?

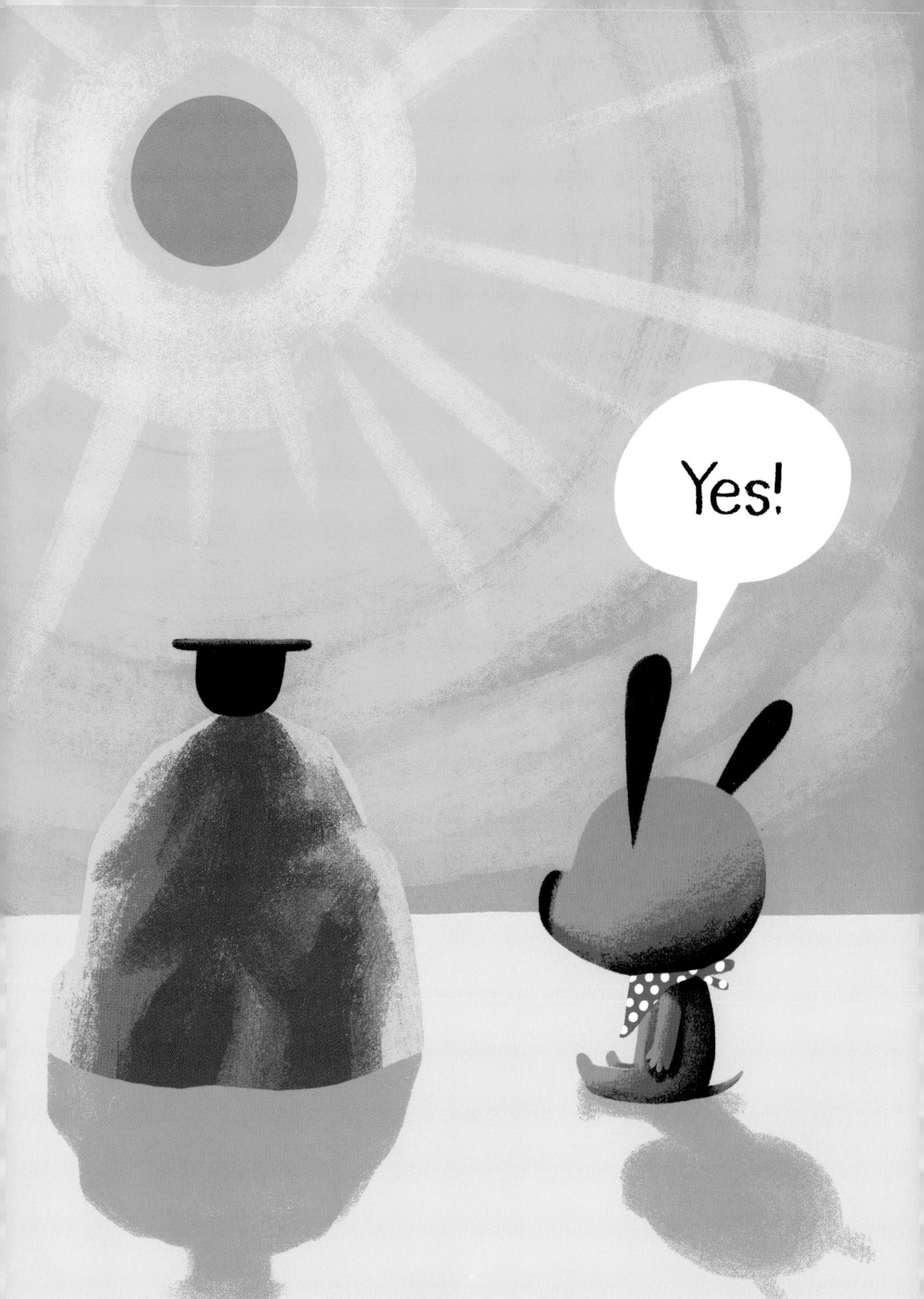
Yes!

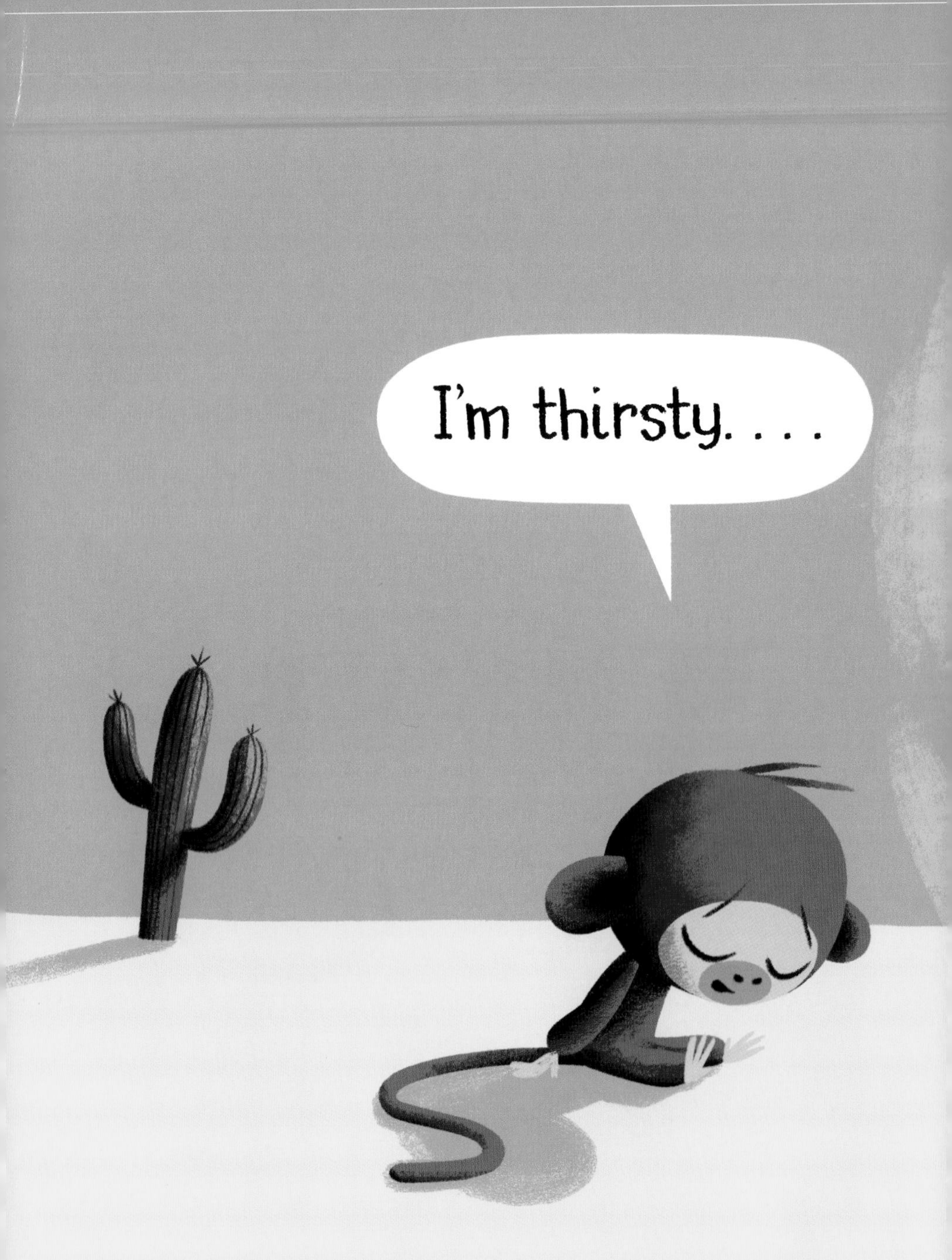
I'm thirsty. . . .

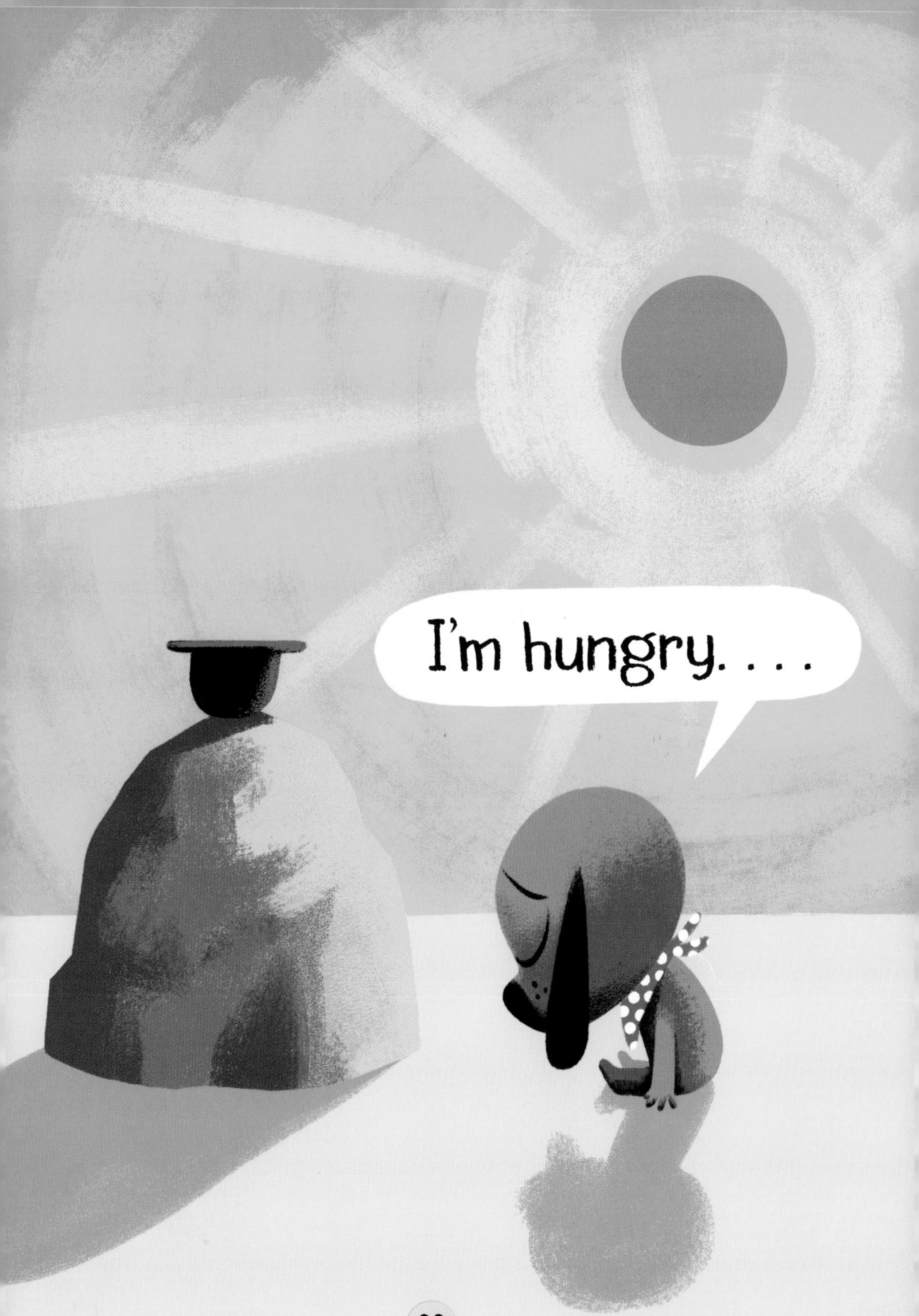
I'm hungry. . . .

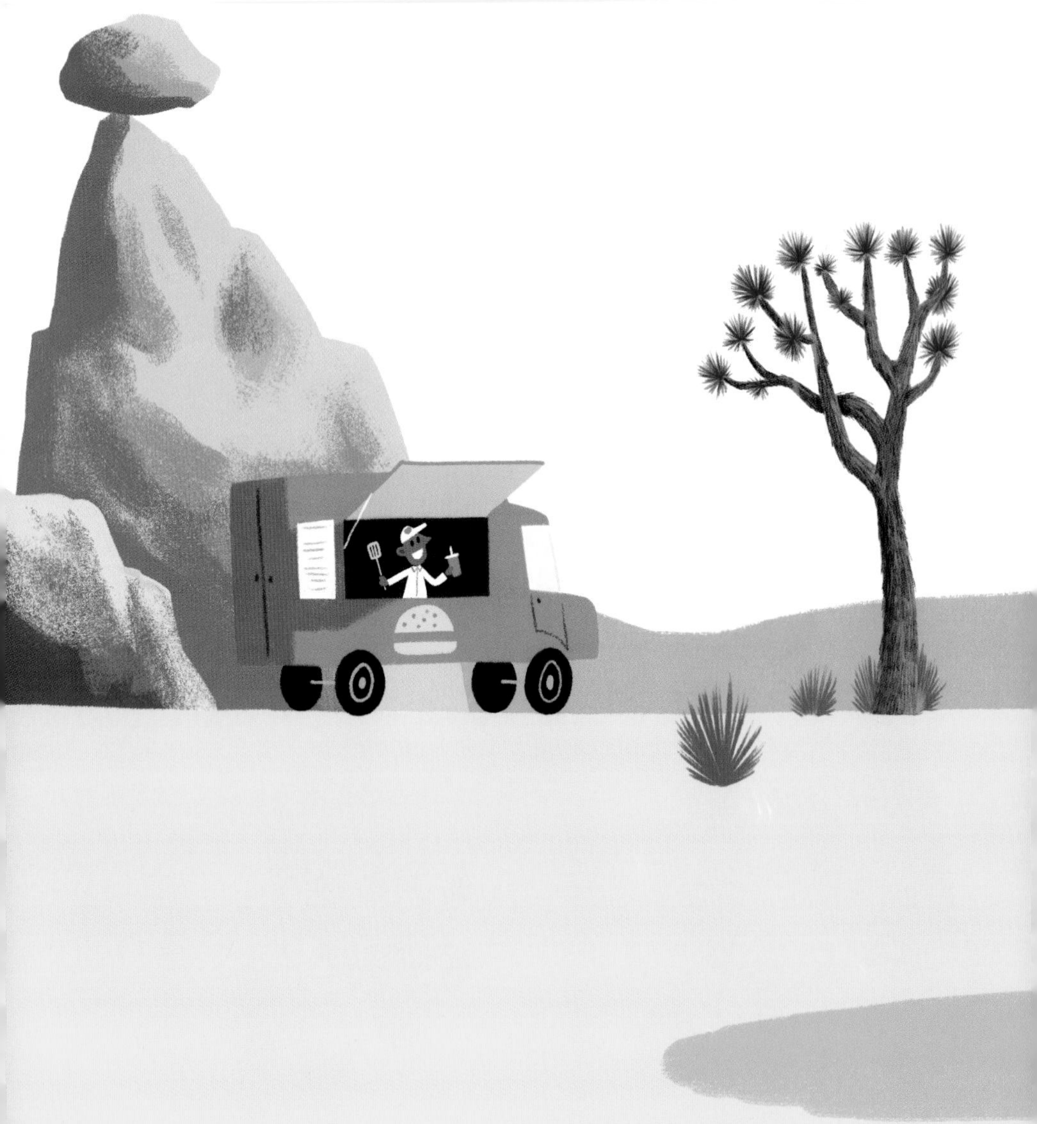

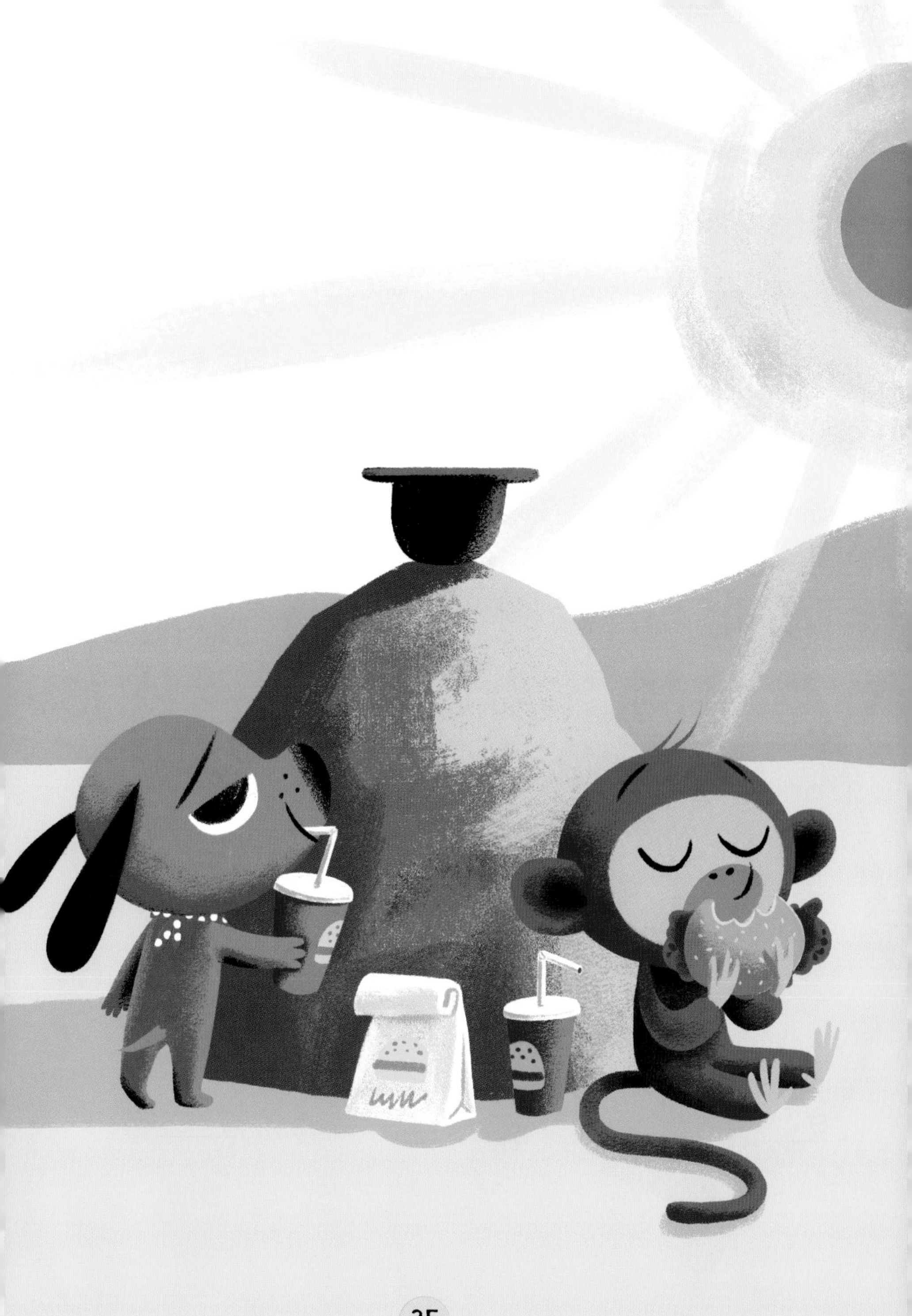

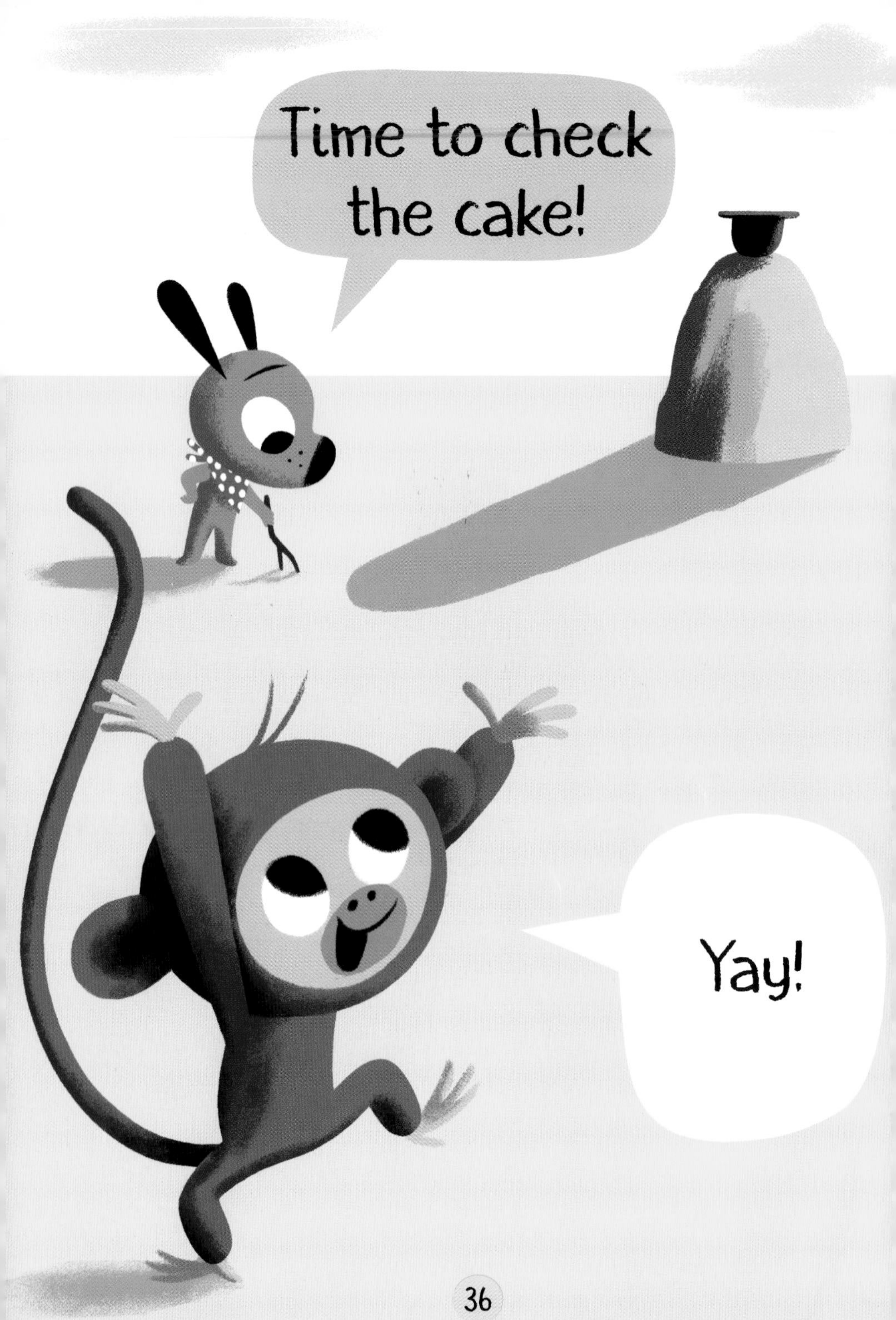
Time to check the cake!
Yay!

Chapter 5
Fake, Fake Cake!

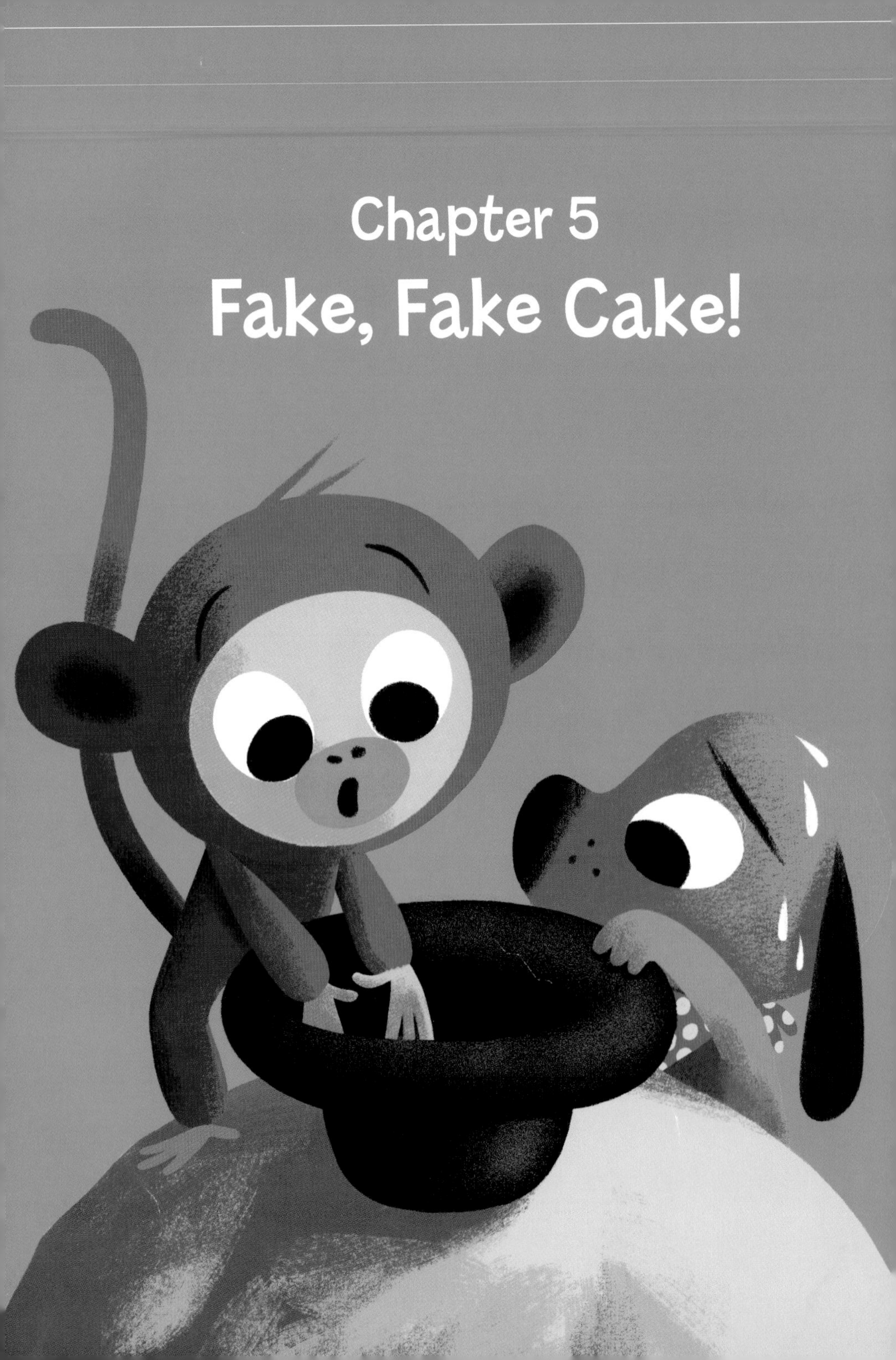

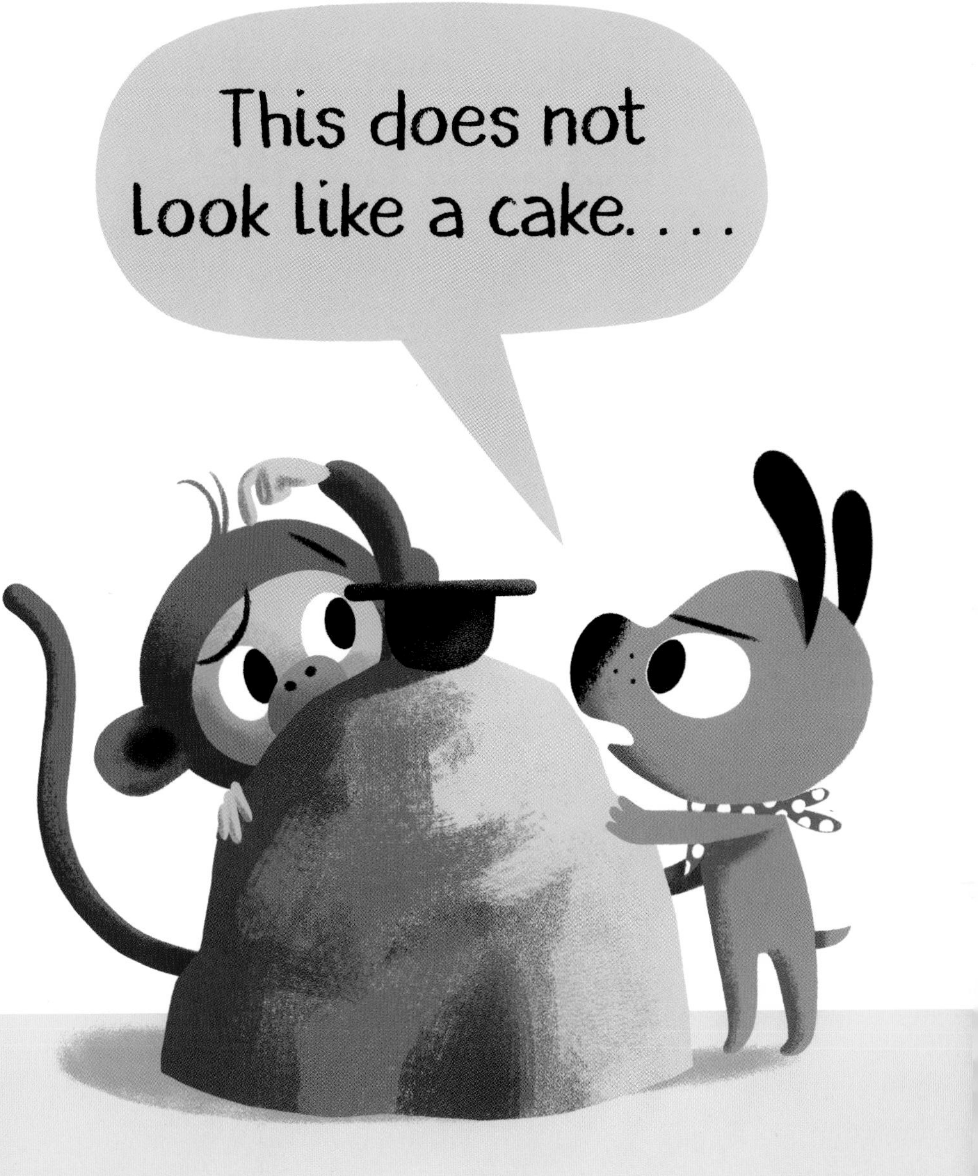
This does not look like a cake. . . .

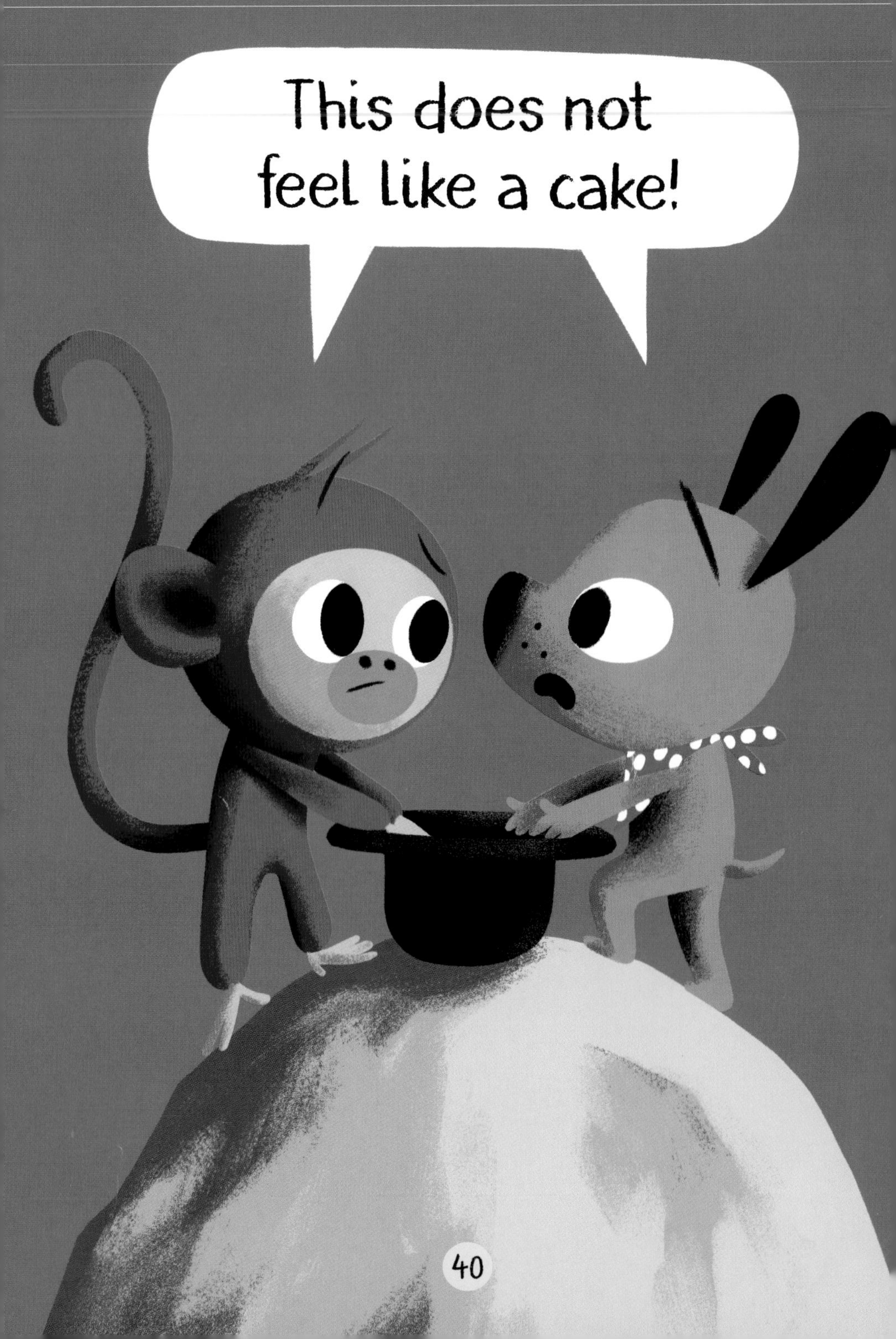
This does not feel like a cake!

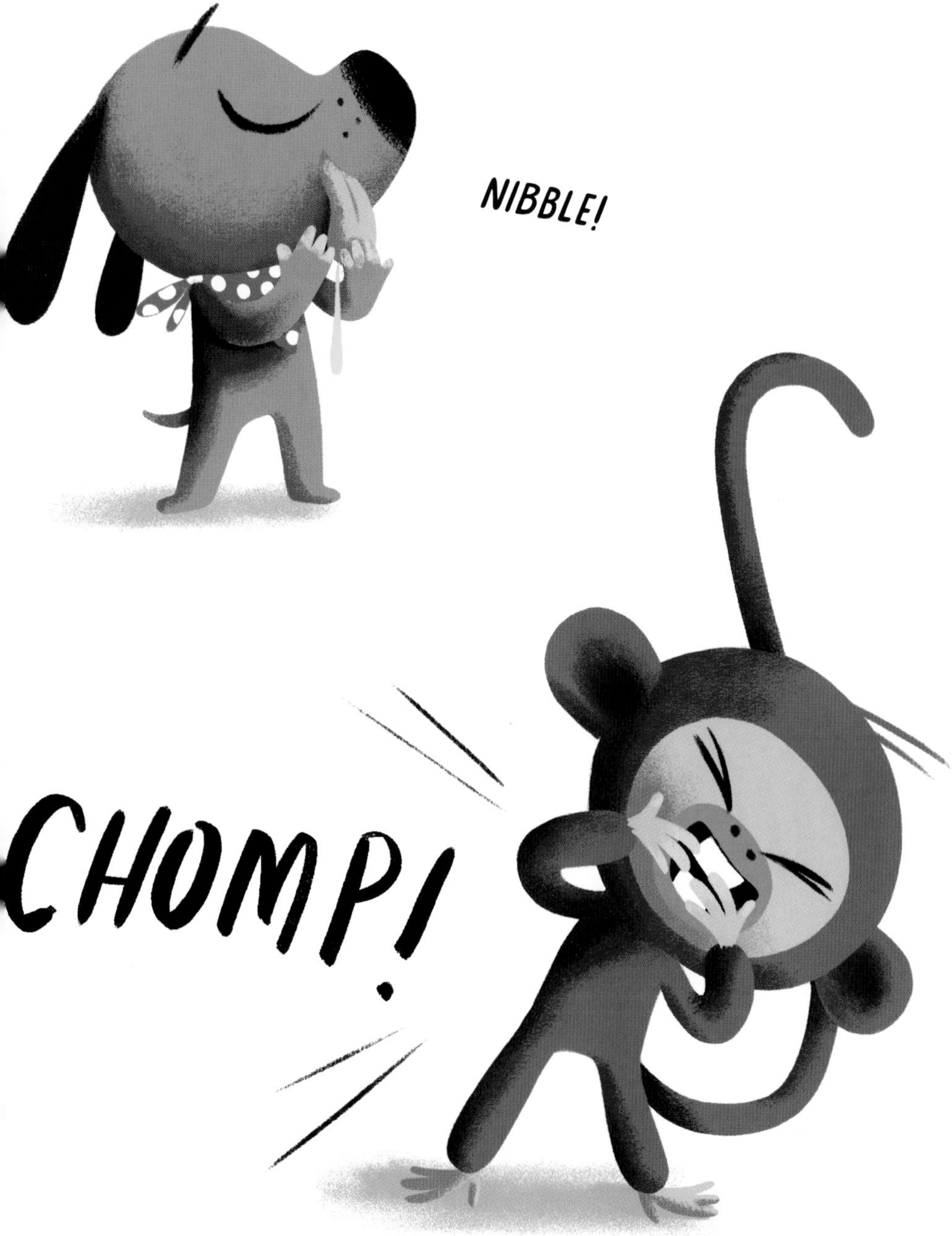
NIBBLE!
CHOMP!

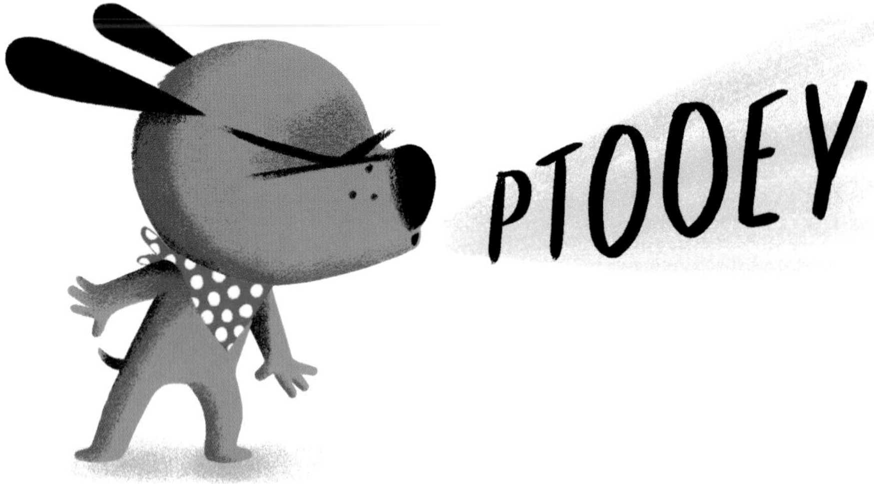
PTOOEY

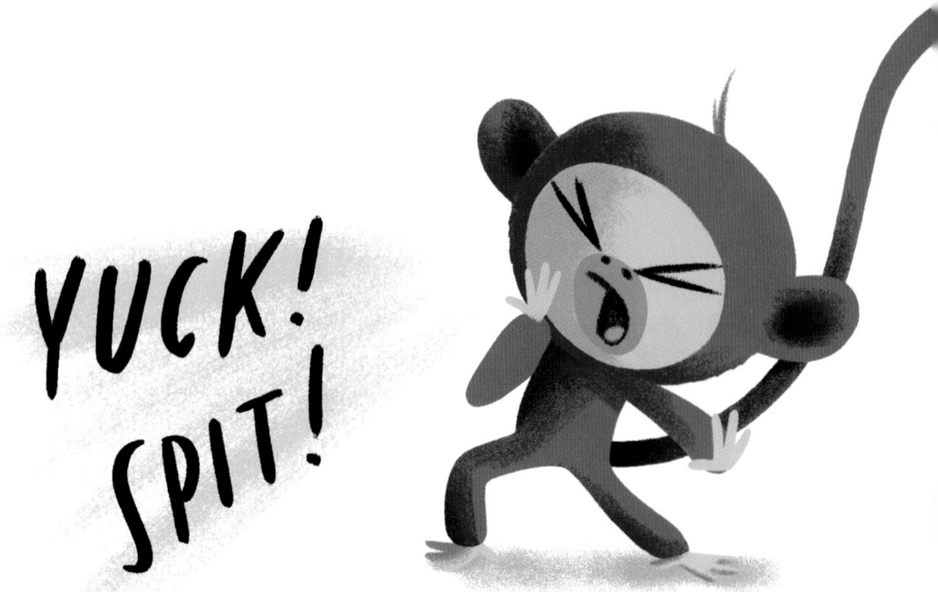
YUCK!
SPIT!

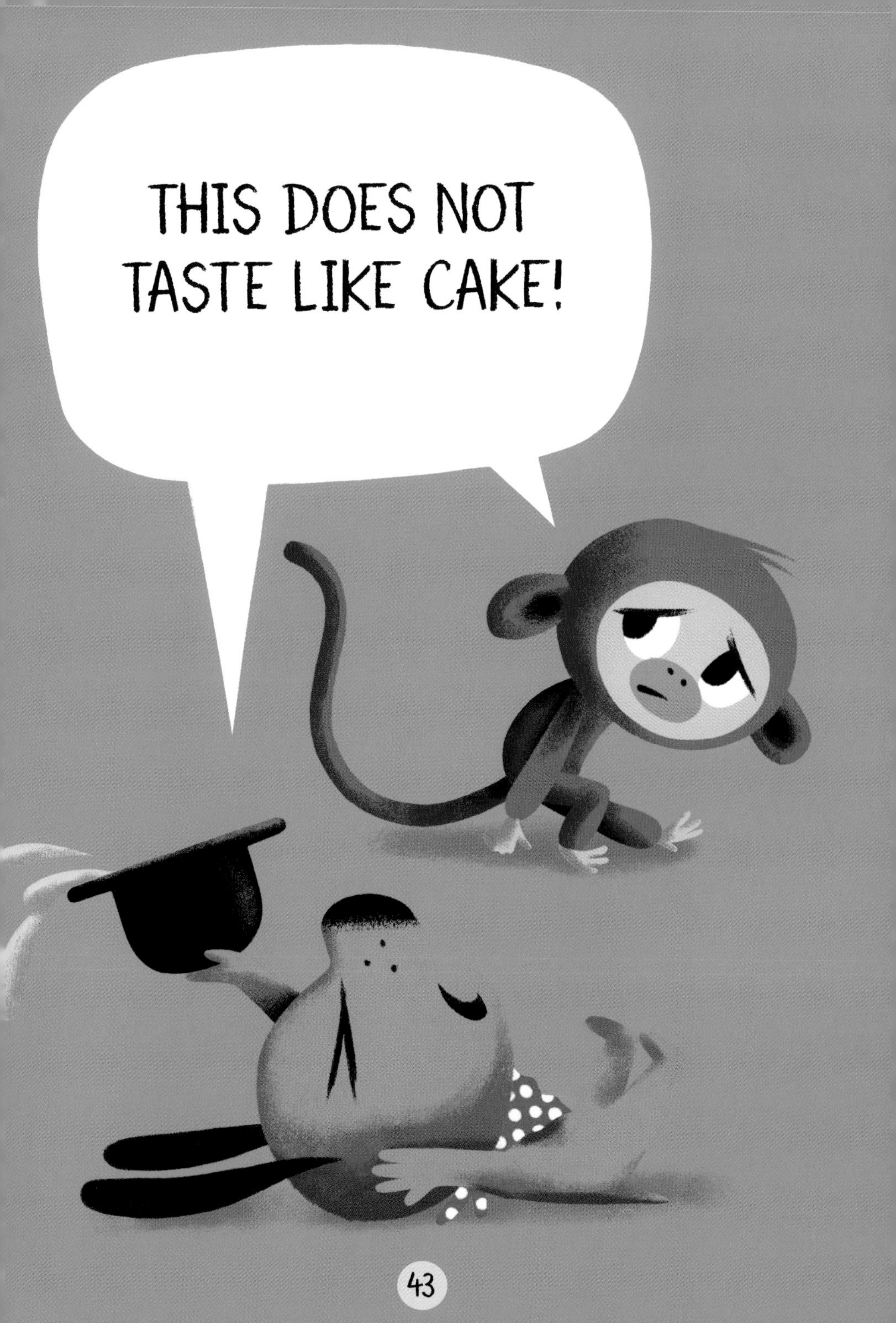
THIS DOES NOT TASTE LIKE CAKE!

Chapter 6
Fun, Fun Cake!

We have failed to make a cake.

Yes. . . .

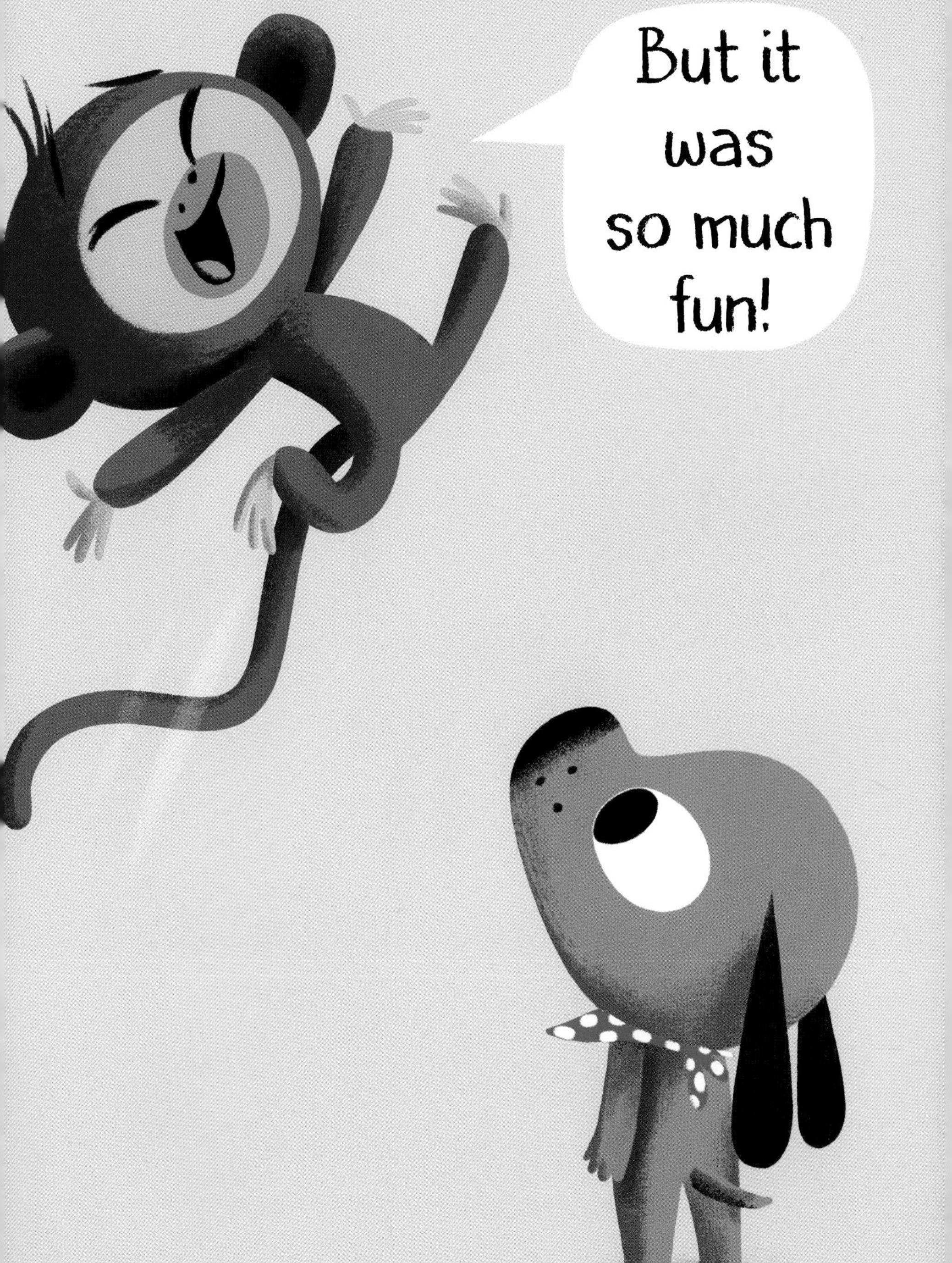
But it was so much fun!

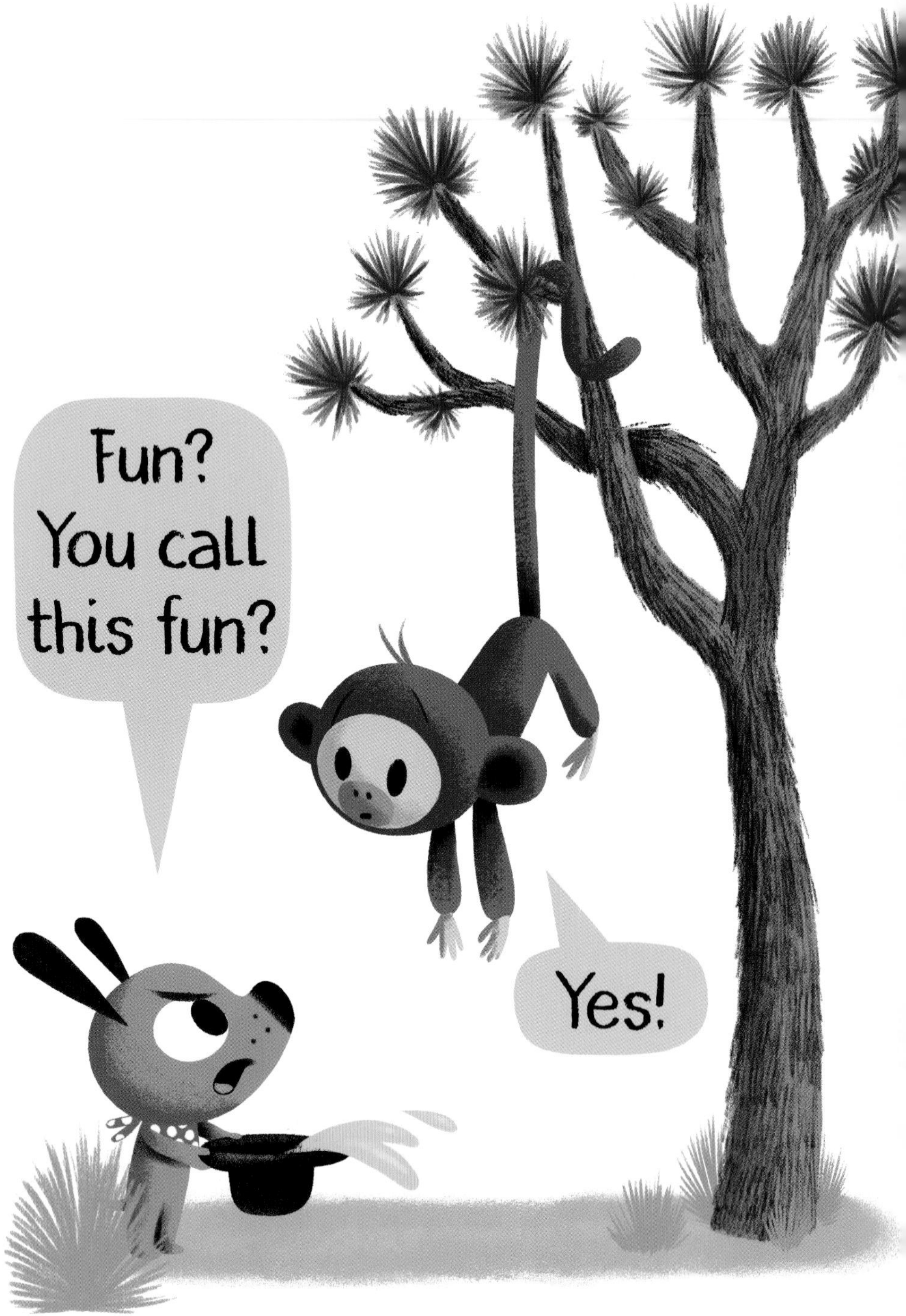
Fun?
You call
this fun?
Yes!

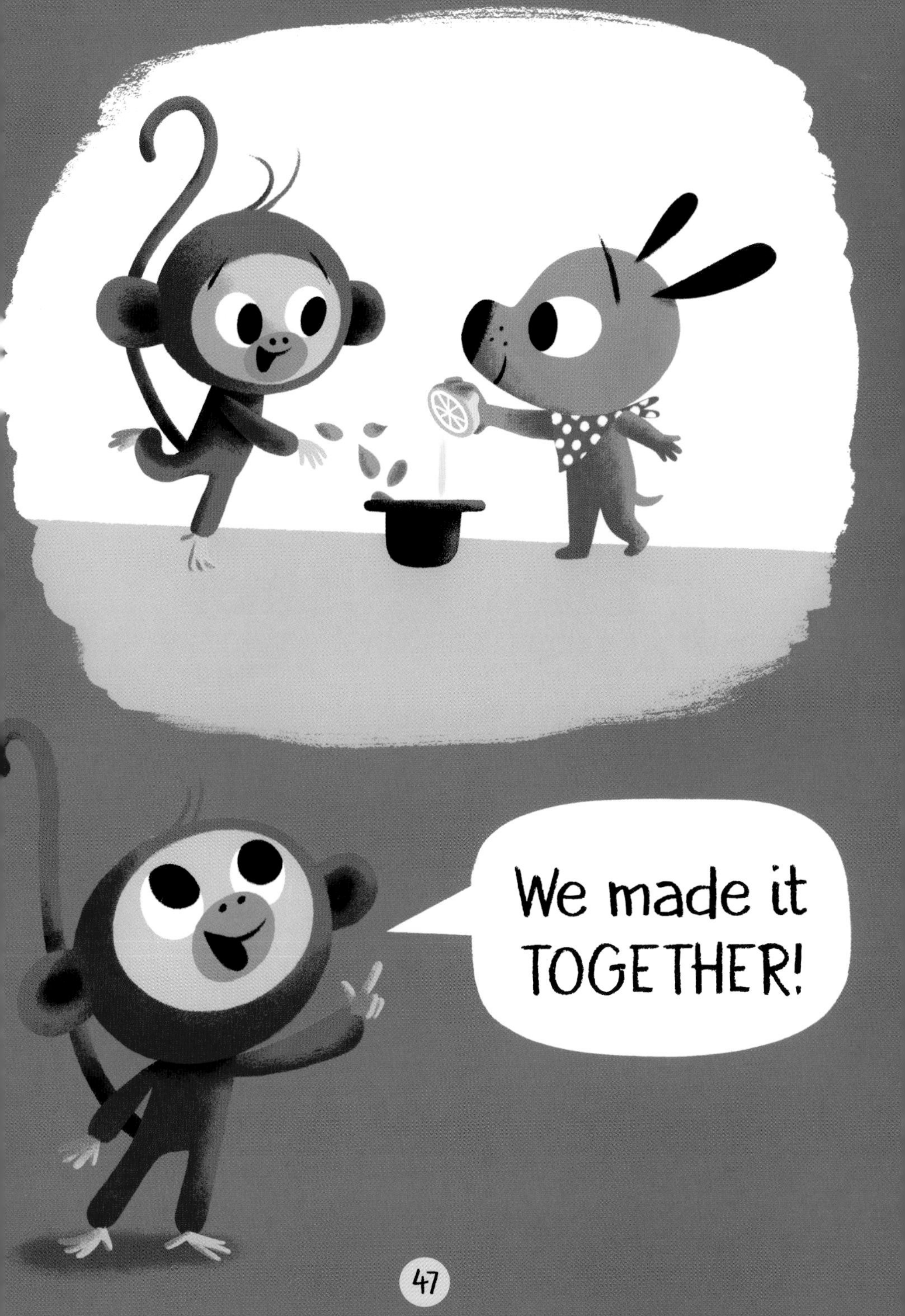
We made it TOGETHER!

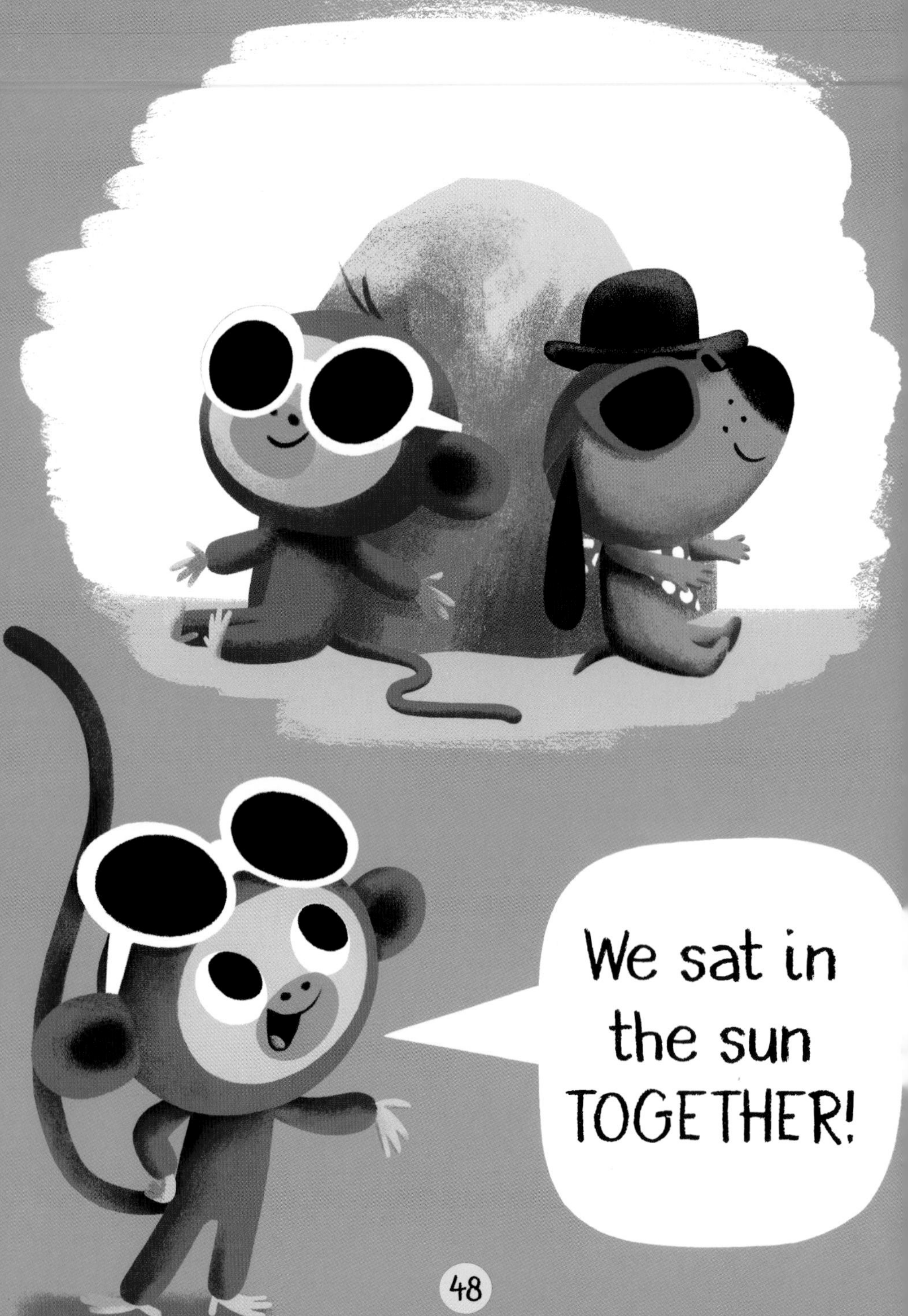
We sat in the sun TOGETHER!

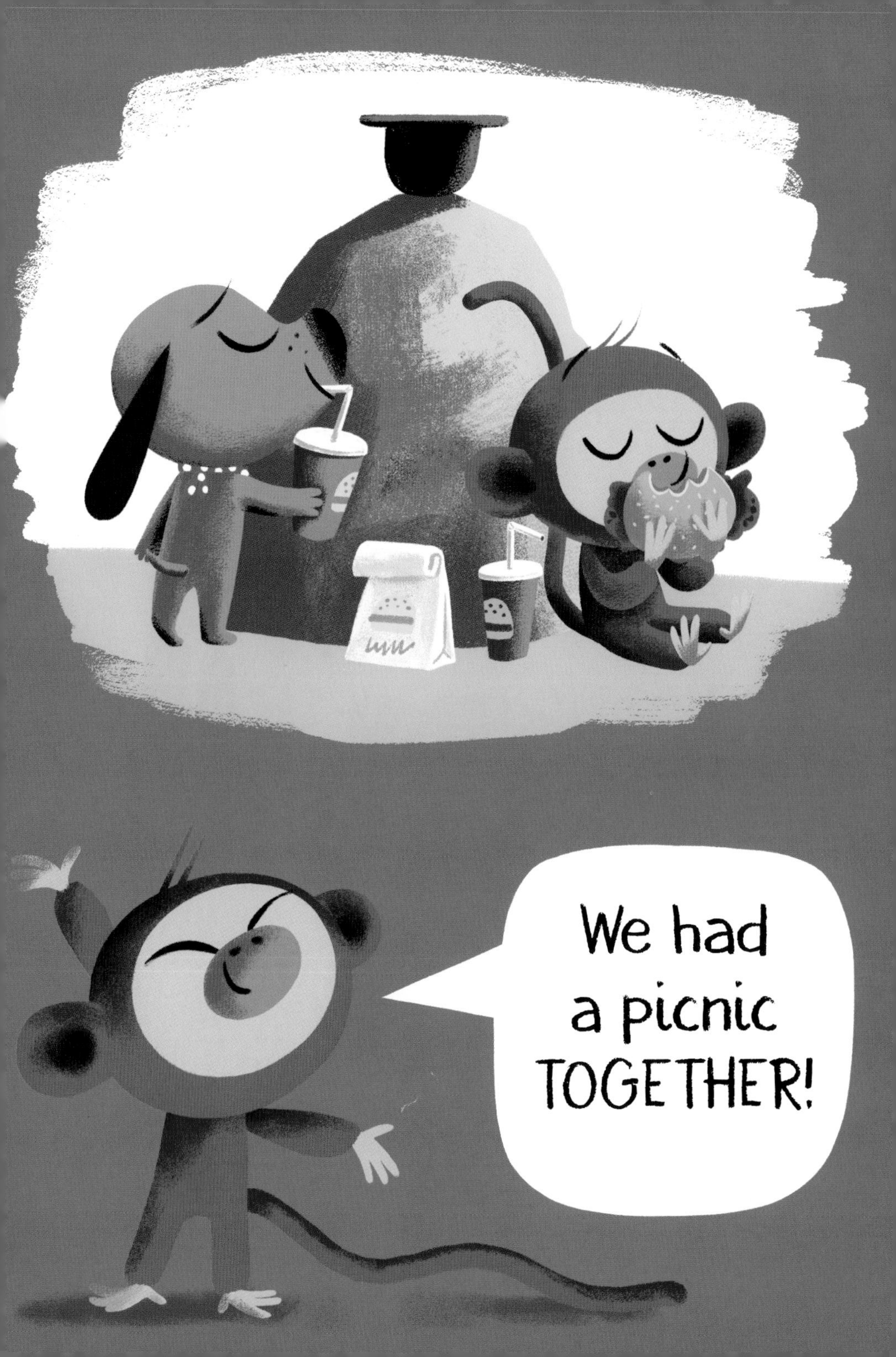
We had a picnic TOGETHER!

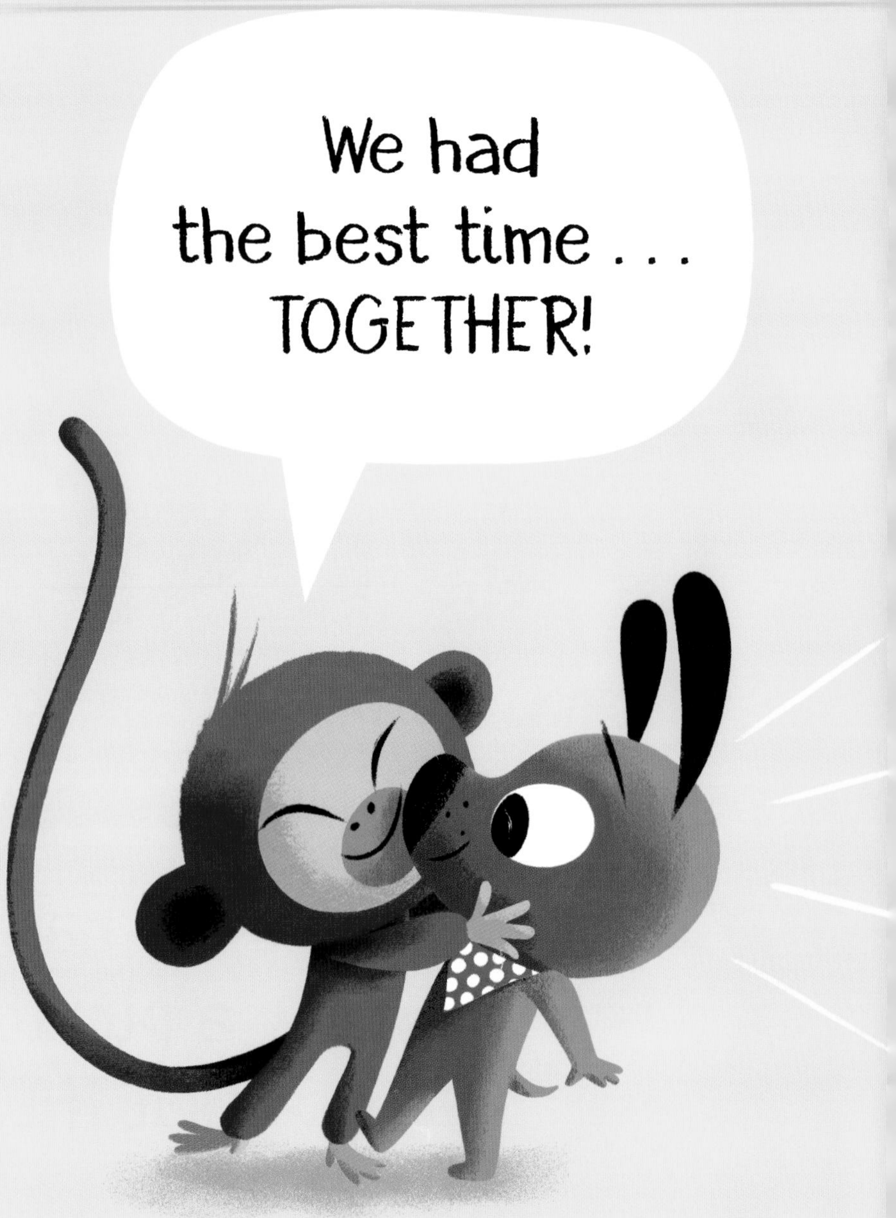
We had
the best time . . .
TOGETHER!

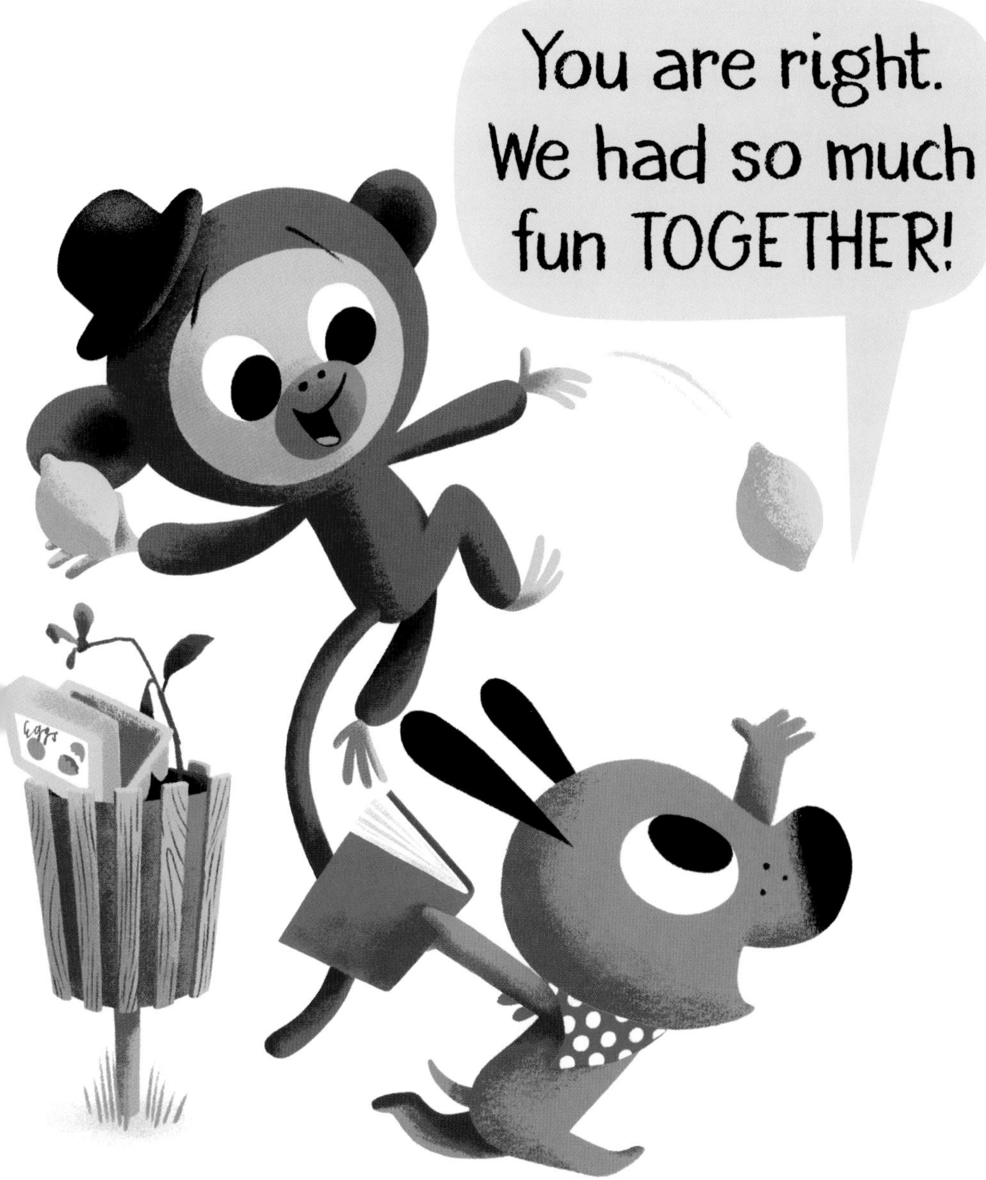
You are right. We had so much fun TOGETHER!
Eggs

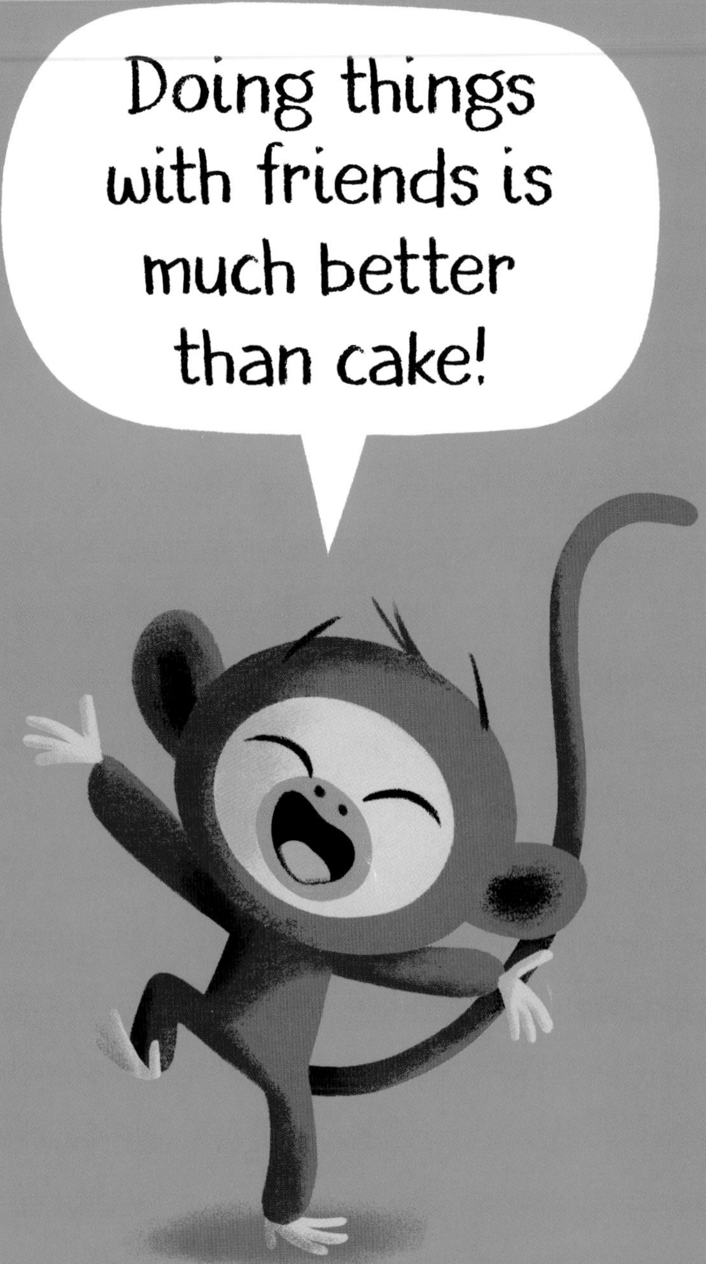
Doing things with friends is much better than cake!

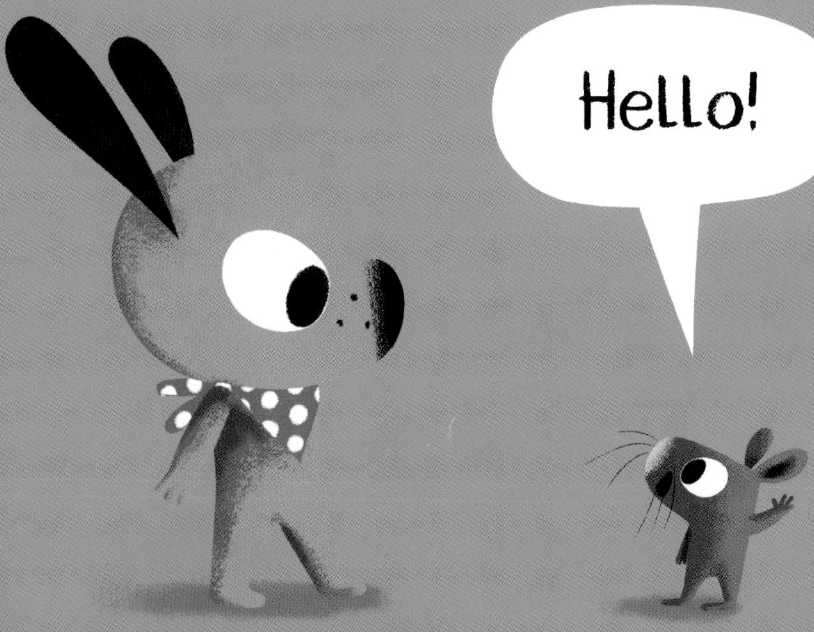
Hello!

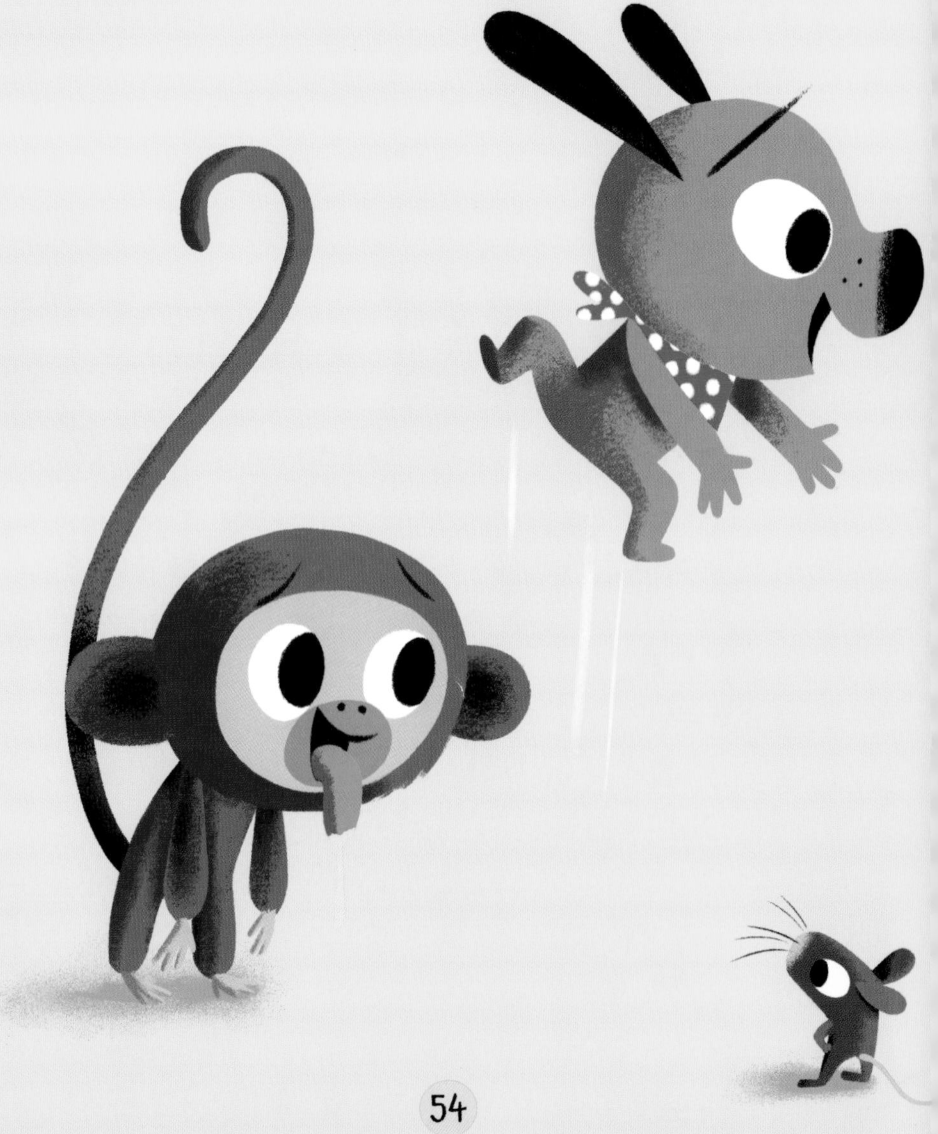

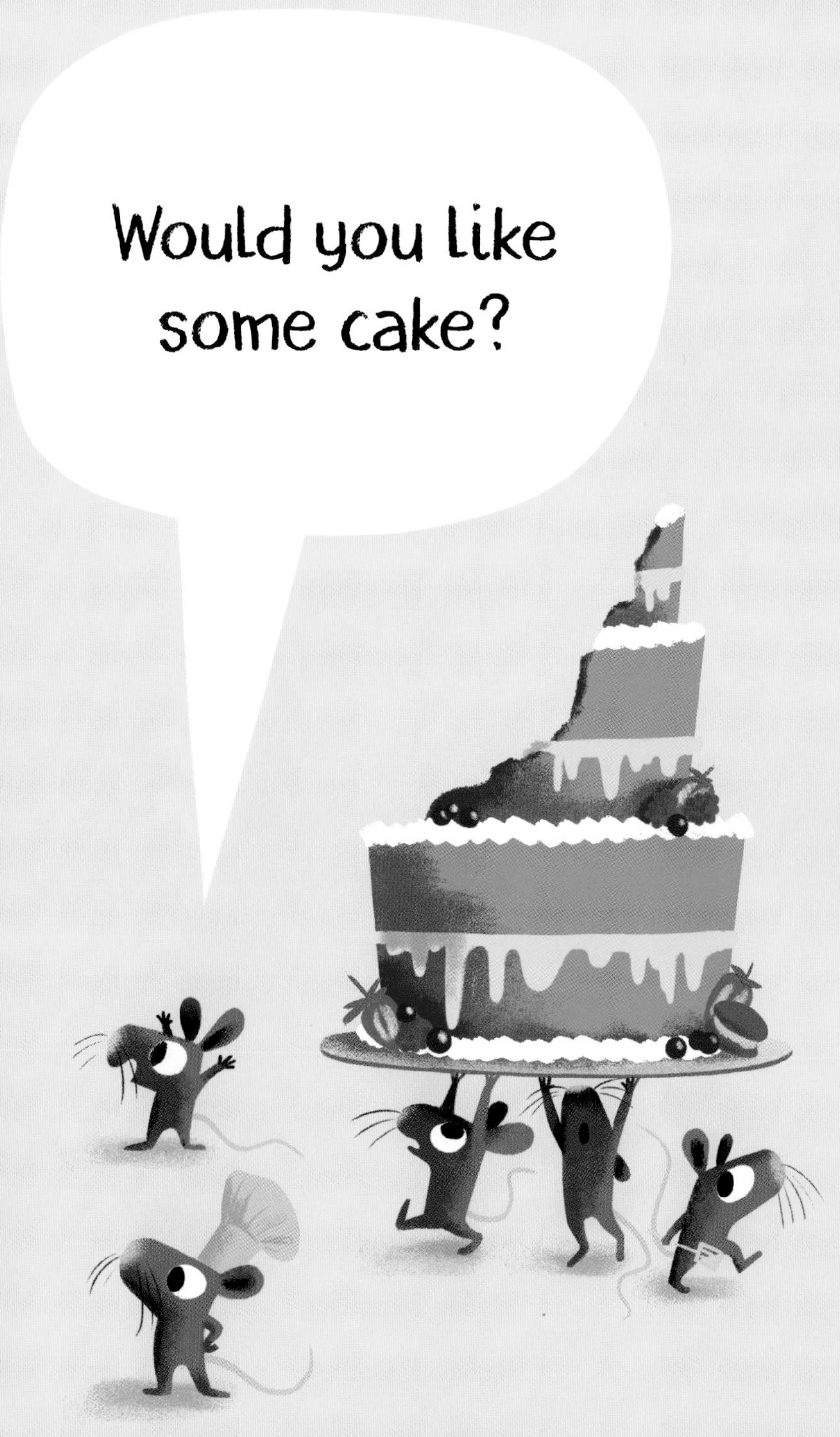
Would you like some cake?

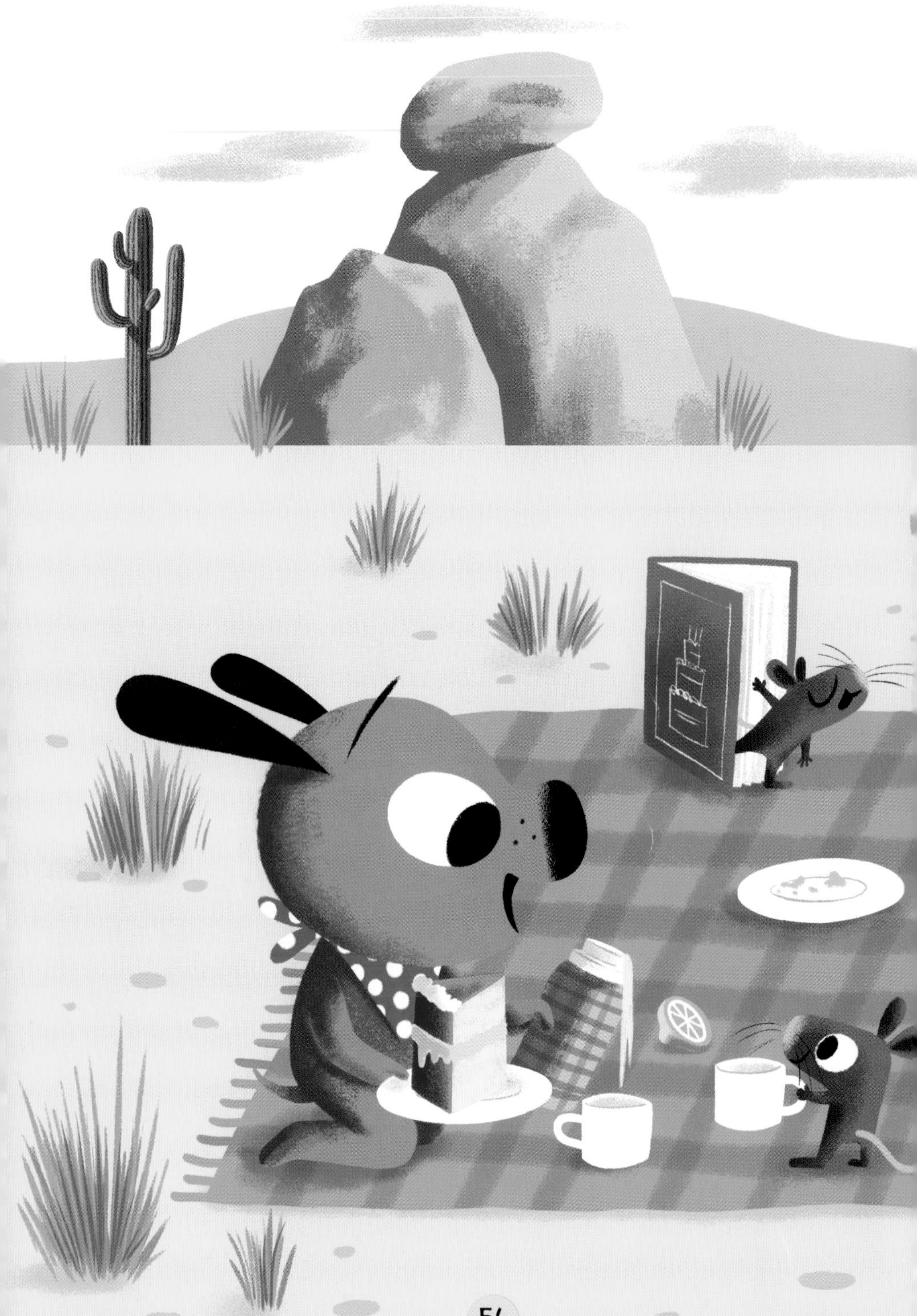

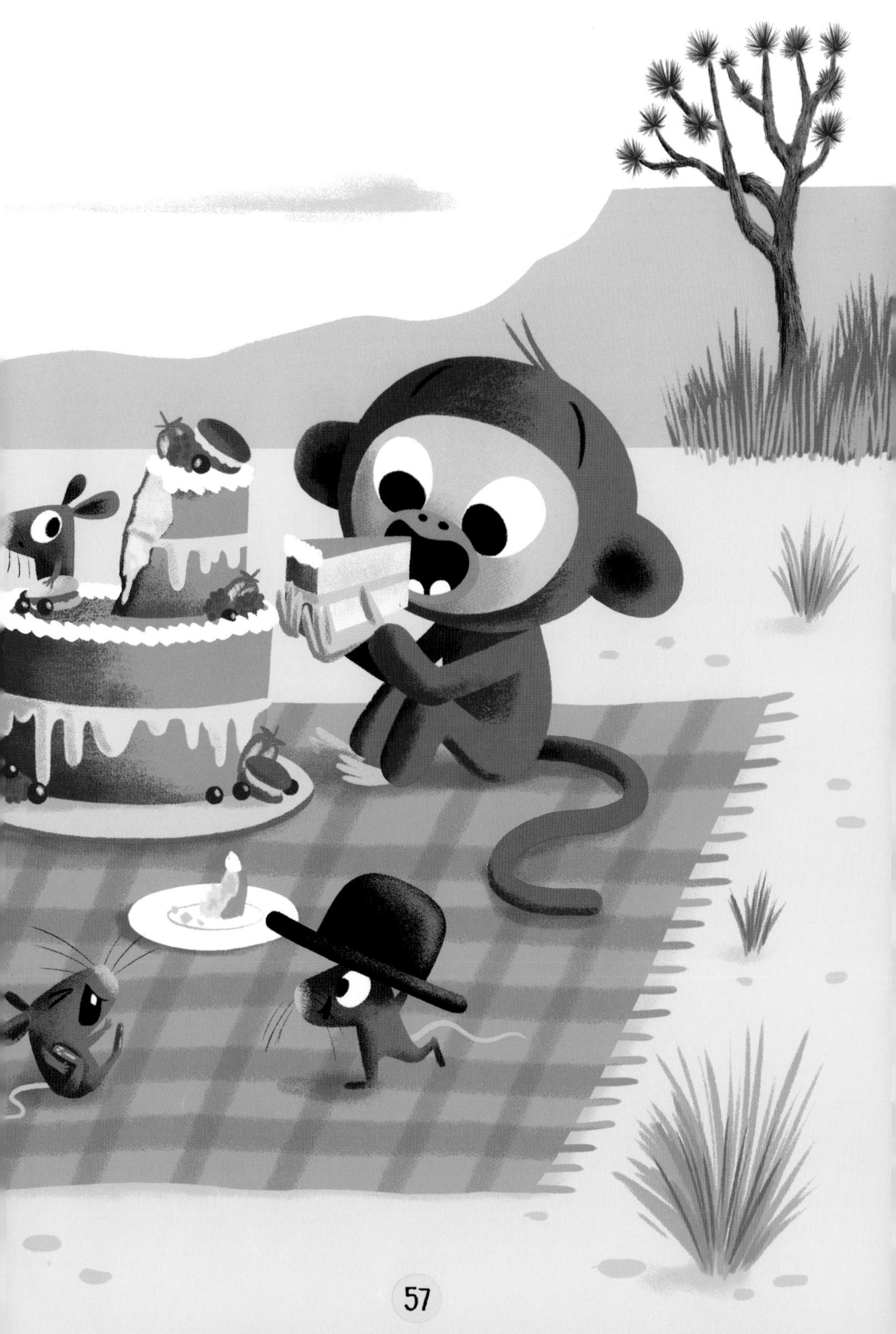

Hungry for another Bobo and Pup-Pup book?

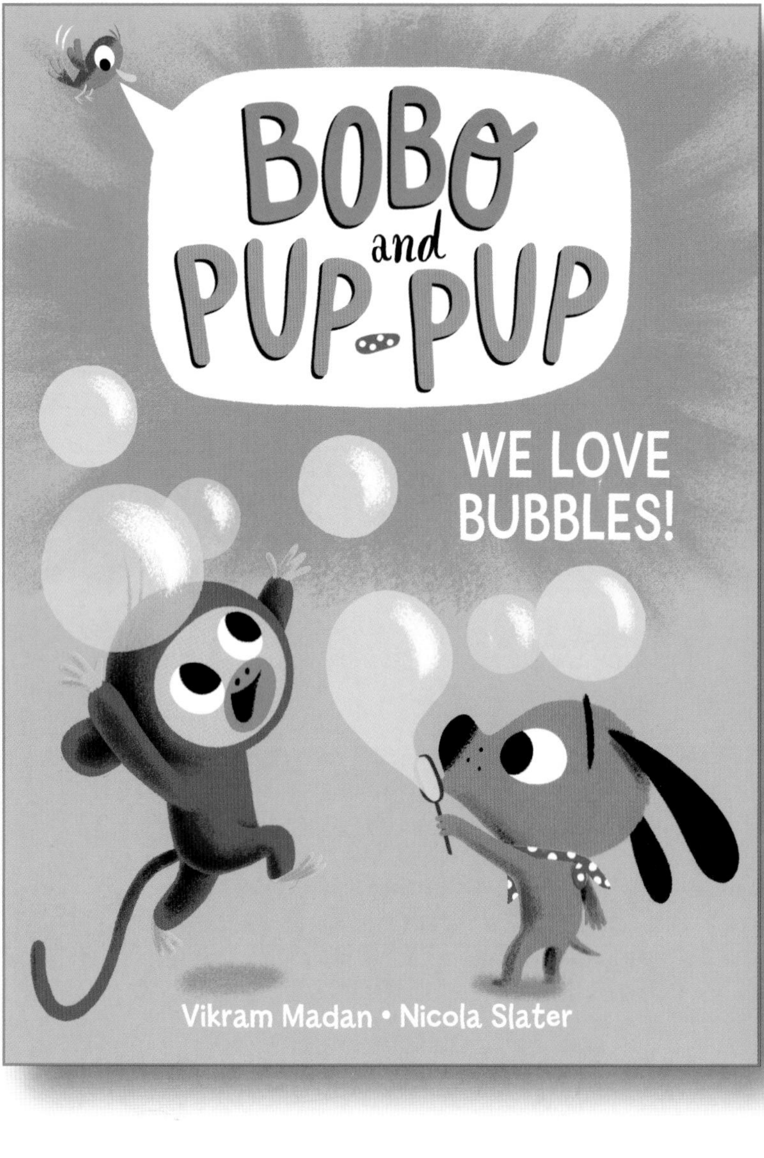
BOBO
and
PUP-PUP
WE LOVE BUBBLES!
Vikram Madan • Nicola Slater

Vikram Madan grew up in India, where he really wanted to be a cartoonist but ended up an engineer. After many years in the tech industry, he finally came to his senses and followed his heart back to humor. He lives near Seattle, where—in addition to making whimsical and humorous visual art—he writes and illustrates books of funny poems, including the *Kirkus Reviews* Best Book *A Hatful of Dragons* and the Moonbeam Award Winners *The Bubble Collector* and *Lord of the Bubbles*. Visit him at VikramMadan.com.

Nicola Slater lives with her family in the wild and windy north of England. She has illustrated many middle-grade novels and picture books, including *Where Is My Pink Sweater?* (which she also wrote), *Leaping Lemmings!, A Skunk in My Bunk!,* and Margaret Wise Brown's *Manners,* a Little Golden Book. In her spare time she likes looking at animals, camping in the rain, and tickling her children. You can follow her on Twitter at @nicolaslater.

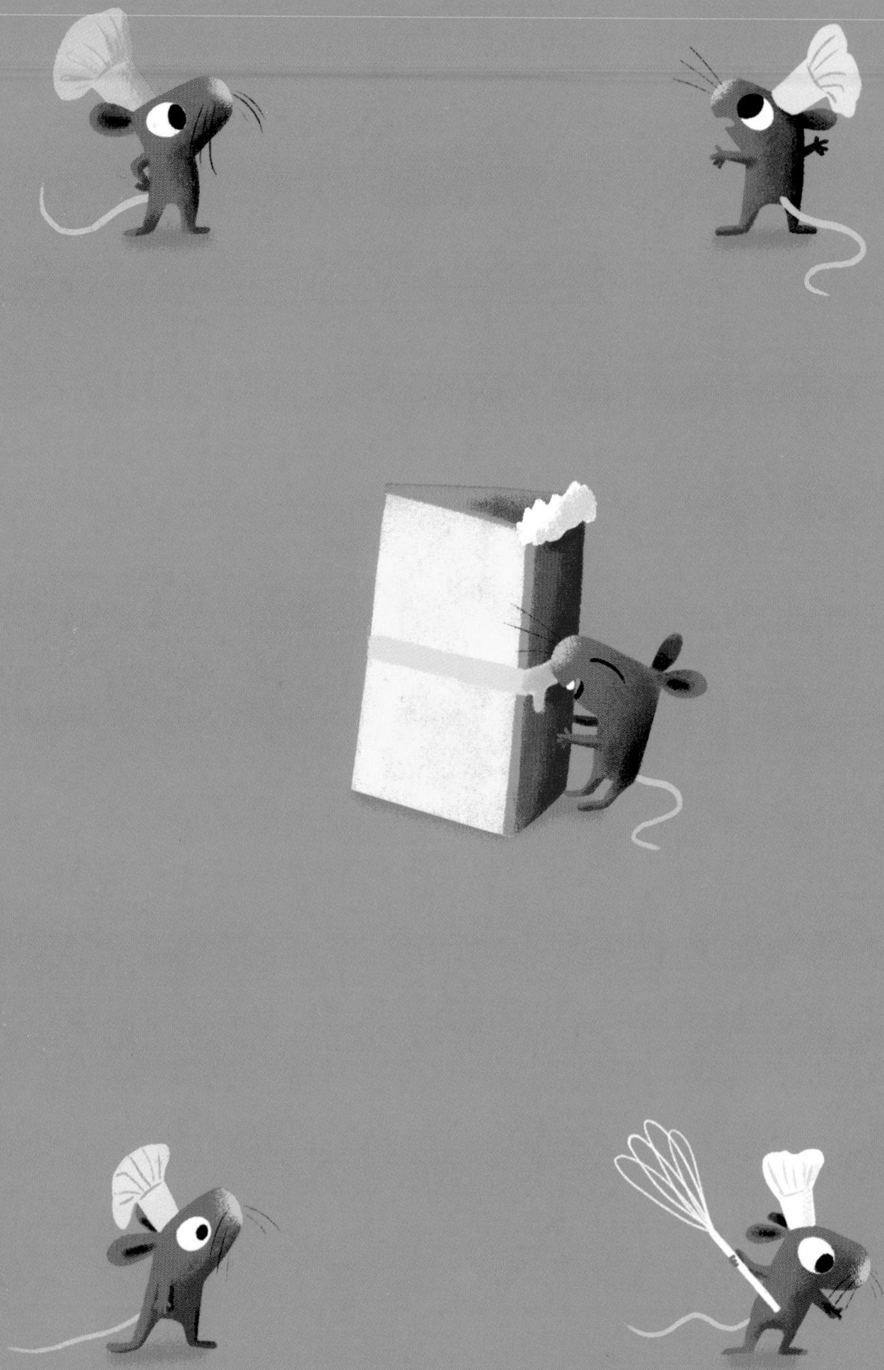